Unwanted in a New World
The New World Book Two

Sherry Derr-Wille

Published by Rogue Phoenix Press, LLP
Copyright © 2021

ISBN: 978-1-62420-604-7

Credits
Cover Artist: Designs by Ms G
Editor: Amanda Armstrong

Dedication

To all of my friends and fans who have believed in me. Also to my husband, bob, who puts up with a crazy writer who often says, "Leave me alone, it's flowing."

Chapter One
Spring 2100

Juanita Little Horse wiped away her tears as she and her boyfriend, Carter Jennings, took the last of her possessions out of her parents' house. Carter was white and although she knew her parents each had whites in their background, they had forbidden her to be with him.

When she could hide the evidence of her pregnancy no longer, she broke the news to her parents. Their immediate response was that she was no longer welcome in their home.

"You were taught better than to give into the demands of the first man to pay you any attention," her father accused. "You are no longer a daughter of mine. If this man is so important to you, he can have you."

She'd turned to her mother for support only to be met with a cold, hard stare.

"Fine," she shouted, as she started packing her belongings. "This is your grandchild, but you will never see him. We're going far away from here."

Carter helped her load the last of her belongings into the cargo area of the hover craft. Once everything was secured, they took their seats and prepared for lift off.

With sadness, she looked back at the only home she'd ever known. She thought perhaps her parents would at least wave good-bye to her, but she was mistaken. The front yard of their neat home was empty. Even her younger brother and sister were conveniently out of sight.

"Don't cry, honey. We can crash at my place until we know where we want to settle. It's not as big as your parents' house, but it's in a good neighborhood. I have a lead on a job in Colorado. They said they'd let me know by the end of the week and we can say good-bye to Montana forever. It will be the two of us against the world."

"What about your parents?"

"I told you, they are no longer with us."

Juanita's tears flowed faster. "It must be the pregnancy. I'm usually not someone to cry at the drop of a hat."

She paused and suddenly remembered something. "I-I don't have my identification. I was in such a hurry. I didn't have time to look for my birth certificate. I have no way to prove who I am. We have to go back and get it."

"Do you know how far we've come? If we turn back now, we won't get to my apartment in Sundance until well after dark. This is an old enough model craft that the night vision doesn't work for shit."

Panicked, Juanita reached for the controls, sending the hover craft into a tailspin.

~ * ~

Sirens screamed through the night as emergency craft converged on the Laughlin Ranch, located at the southeast corner of the state of Montana.

"I saw it go down," Pete Laughlin said. "It looked like the pilot lost control and it went into a spin before it crashed, right here in the middle of my cow pasture. From what I could tell, there were only two people in it."

"It looks like the man is dead, but he's so badly burned, I don't know if anyone could identify him, Sheriff," the first medical tech on the scene reported. "I don't know how it happened, but the girl was thrown away from the fire. She's still alive, but probably not for long. She's also pregnant. If we want to save the baby, we'll have to transport her to the closest hospital as soon as possible."

The captain in charge agreed and watched as the rescuers secured her into the ambulance. He wanted to go with her and see if she could give him some sort of a statement as to how the accident occurred. Instead, he knew he needed to stay behind and try to figure out who these people were.

Debris was spread across the lush, green pasture. Checking it out, he decided one or both of them were in the process of moving to a different location.

"Who are you?" Sheriff Collins asked, knowing full well he wouldn't receive an answer.

Turning to one of the officers with him he asked, "Were you able to get a VIN on the craft?"

"Everything was burned too badly. How the girl survived is anyone's guess. If you ask me, I'd say this was a stolen vehicle, but who would steal something this old? The damn thing shouldn't have been flying in the first place."

"From the looks of things, they were just kids. The girl couldn't have been anywhere near her twentieth birthday. It's a shame, a damn dirty shame."

~ * ~

The emergency room of the country hospital buzzed with activity. Dr. Christopher Parker got the call about a hover craft accident on a remote ranch several miles away from the hospital. He wasn't looking forward to receiving the sole survivor of the crash. From the report he'd received, his patient was a young woman who was at least seven months pregnant. The prognosis didn't sound good. It was entirely possible he would lose two patients before the night was over.

The air ambulance arrived and two med techs wheeled in a young woman lying motionless on the gurney.

Dr. Parker wasted no time in examining his patient. Although her skin color was fair, he could see her blood matted hair was originally dark black and her high cheek bones denoted a Native American heritage in her lineage.

It was evident she wouldn't last the night, but there was a fetal heartbeat. He knew he had to do his best to save this tiny life. Calling up to the operating room he made the arrangements for a Caesarean section to be done to deliver the child.

An hour later, he received word the child had been born, but the mother had perished. Being so premature, the baby boy weighed only one pound, eleven and a half ounces. It was entirely possible he wouldn't survive the night.

"Do you know the name of the mother?" the nurse who approached him asked.

"From what the police have told me, neither the boy nor the girl had any identification. I know we have to name him something. I'll give him my first name and since the accident happened on the Laughlin Ranch, why don't we name him Christopher Laughlin? It won't matter because I'm certain the boy won't make it through tonight, to say nothing of growing to adulthood."

~ * ~

Six months later, Dr. Parker received a call from the neonatal unit that Christopher was ready to be released from the hospital. Over the past six months, he'd visited the unit often checking on the baby he'd saved when he couldn't do the same thing for his mother.

The vision of the dying young mother and the premature baby who didn't have a snowball's chance in hell of surviving came to mind. It was a night he would never forget no matter how many days, weeks, months or years passed.

"Who are you going to release him to?" he finally asked.

"Since he has no parents and we know of no other family, we're sending him to Henderson Ranch in Nevada. They take in unadoptable children."

Dr. Parker was confused. "Why is he unadoptable?"

"Don't you know? No agencies want to deal in mixed breed children. His DNA came back and his origins are Cheyenne and European. The Cheyenne don't want him and there's not a couple listed in the system who want to take on someone like him. With his mother being Native American and his father completely unknown, it's a risk to say the very least. It was the thought of the officers at the scene that the hover craft the parents were flying in when the crash happened was stolen. Of course, with the Vin number burned off, there was no way to verify their assumptions. Would you want to adopt a child with that kind of a background? Henderson Ranch is the best place for him."

Dr. Parker tended to agree with the nurse, but he felt sorry for the child who would grow up without the love of his parents. At this point in his life, he wasn't able to even think of adopting a child. He and his wife had three children. Between his busy schedule at the hospital and her position at a prestigious accounting firm, there was no time to take on what could turn out to become a very troubled child. It was for the best if he was sent somewhere equipped to handle such children.

Chapter Two
2118

"You'll be turning eighteen soon, Christopher," his best friend Marco said as they did their chores on the ranch. "What are your plans?"

"Plans? What kind of plans can I make? The only thing I know is carpentry and ranching. It would be different if we were educated, but I can hardly read or write. Who is going to hire someone like me?"

"I heard about a group up in Idaho. It's all young guys, like the two of us. The leader is Patrick Ernst. You have to be careful, though. If they ever learn about your DNA, they won't take you. They call themselves members of the superior race. That means they don't have any Native American blood. You have enough white in you that you could pass. Me on the other hand, would probably be shot on sight. Too much Mexican in me. I'm hoping to go down to Mexico and get a job on one of the ranches down there. With the language decoder chip that was implanted in both of us when we were born, I shouldn't have a problem with the language barrier."

Later that night, Christopher lay on his bunk contemplating the future. As much as he wanted to have a future, he couldn't help thinking of the past.

At birth he'd been deemed to be unadoptable because of his Native American heritage. He had no idea what that meant, but he knew it couldn't be good. The ranch where he'd grown up was full of kids like him. Marco was Mexican and white while there were several kids who were black, yet not completely.

The Henderson's told them that kids like them were no good for anything except manual labor. They certainly didn't deserve to have more than a rudimentary education. He could read, but not very well. He could also do simple math. Who needed those things when their main job on the ranch was herding cattle and taking care of horses? Ever since he was six years old, his days were filled with chores on the ranch that should have been done by adults. Of course, adults would have been expected to be paid. As children, they were told the work they did paid for the care and housing they'd received.

They were also reminded the reason they were there was because they had parents who didn't want them. Christopher always felt a bit superior to the other kids. He'd been brought there because his parents had been killed in a hover craft crash just prior to his birth. From what he'd been told, he had no other family. To be truthful, no one even expected him to live past the first night of his birth. Where his name came from was anyone's guess.

As a child, he'd been sickly, or at least that's what he was told. Mrs. Henderson said the only reason he'd grown into adulthood was because of the hard work he'd done for the past twelve years. He always wondered how much of the story was true.

~ * ~

"I have your things packed," Mrs. Henderson said when he came into the main house for the morning meal. "Today you're eighteen and the state won't be paying us to keep you any longer. I don't care where you go or what you do, but you can't stay here."

Although Christopher knew this day was coming, he was caught unawares. Never before in his life had he been told when his birthday was, only that he was this age or that age. He knew his eighteenth birthday would be coming soon. He just didn't know when it would be.

Along with his belongings, Mrs. Henderson gave him a hundred dollars. He had no idea what to do with the money. In all his life, he'd never handled money and didn't know what it was worth.

Before any of the other kids came in for the morning meal, Mr. Henderson took him to the nearest town and dropped him off. He knew it was because they didn't want the other kids to know he was leaving. Over the past eighteen years he'd experienced older and even younger kids disappear with no knowledge why they left or where they went.

With nowhere to go, he stood in front of what might be a store. He'd heard about them, but had never set foot off the ranch before and didn't know what it was.

"You one of them kids from out at Henderson's place?" a middle-aged man asked him.

"How did you know?" Christopher inquired.

"A couple of times a year, old man Henderson brings one of you kids into town and drops them off without a pot to piss in or a window to throw it out of. Let me guess, they gave you a hundred dollars. Considering what they get from the state for all of the kids who are out there, this is just a drop in the bucket. It won't get you anywhere. To be truthful, it will hardly get you a meal and some clothes."

"So, what am I supposed to do? I was told I should go to see someone named Patrick Ernst in Idaho, but I don't even know where that is or how to get there." Christopher blessed his good memory for being able to remember the name and location of the man Marco told him about.

"You could do worse than hooking up with Ernst and his bunch. At least you'd get three hots' and a cot without having to be locked up by the authorities."

"I don't understand what that means," Christopher replied, completely confused.

"Let me try to explain. From what I've heard, Henderson didn't give you any formal education. What you probably do know is carpentry, which is a lost art, and ranching. Ernst's group are freedom fighters. I only know about them because his pa and me grew up together. I can't say I completely agree with what they're doing, but at least they won't ask any questions about your background. They don't care if you can read or write. It's grunt work, but I hear they provide you with clothes and you get three good meals a day. For now, why don't you come home with me. Won't be the first time I've brought one of Henderson's boys' home for a good meal. I can get in contact with my friend and he can reach his son. The missus won't mind. She likes to be of help just like me."

"I don't know you and you don't know me."

"I go by the name of Pops but my real name is Paul Granger, the wife is Doreen. What's your name?"

"Christopher, Christopher Laughlin. Don't know where I came from or who my family is. I've never lived anywhere other than the ranch. They gave me papers that told me about who I am, but I don't know what they mean."

"We'll sort all of that out. Come along with me, Christopher. I'll send word to Doreen to expect us."

With no other options, Christopher went with Pops to a modest home situated on one of the side streets of the town.

~ * ~

Doreen Granger hurried to ready the spare room. This wasn't the first time her husband brought home one of the Henderson boys. She ached for these young men, but not enough to keep them from the destiny they needed to fulfill. The treatment they received out at that so-called orphanage was an outrage, but who was she to pass judgement? The least she could do was to give them a good meal and a place to stay until they could be placed elsewhere. Some of them needed to get to Mexico to work on one of the ranches there, others wanted to find their families, or went off to join other groups of young men and women who banded together to make their own way in the world.

She heard the front door open and hurried to meet the newest young man to cross her path.

"You must be Christopher," she said, extending her hand. "I'm Doreen, but you can call me Ma. Pops will show you to your room and where you can wash up. I have supper on the stove. If I don't miss my guess, they kicked you out before you could have your morning meal. Well, you won't have to worry about that here. There's always plenty to eat at my table and I don't abide with anyone going without a meal."

The look on Christopher's face was one of bewilderment. "Thank you, Ma'am. I don't know how I will be able to repay you."

"Don't think of that now. Until you decide what you want to do,

Pops and I can use your help around the house. If I'm not mistaken, you have some carpentry skills. Goodness knows, there's plenty of projects around here. Pops isn't what anyone would call a carpenter. He makes a good living but around the house, he's worthless."

"I don't understand, what's a good living?"

Doreen ached at what this young man didn't understand.

"What Ma is saying is, I have a good job. I go to work every day Monday through Friday. This being the weekend, it's my time to go into town and see what kind of trouble I can get into."

"What's a job?"

Doreen could feel tears of frustration welling behind her eyes. She listened intently as her husband explained about his job at the Hover Craft Factory and how he received a salary for the work he did. Knowing what she did about the kids out at Henderson's place, she understood his confusion about working and making money. Those kids were little more than slave labor and when they were too old for the state to compensate the Henderson's for their work, they were kicked out to try to make their way in a world they couldn't begin to understand.

~ * ~

Christopher was surprised by the room Pops and Ma allowed him to stay in. All his life, he'd lived in a dormitory with nine other boys. He'd gone from the lower bunk to the top when he turned thirteen, at least that's how old Mrs. Henderson said he was.

"What should I do with this money?" he asked Pops.

"You can put it in that top dresser drawer for safe keeping. While you're here, you won't be needing it."

Christopher did as he was told and put the five crisp twenty-dollar bills in the top drawer of the dresser. He hoped when the time came for him to use it, someone would tell him what to do with it.

The food on Ma's table was the best he'd ever eaten. Unlike the slop he'd grown up eating. There was meat, real meat, not just something that came from a can. The vegetables were also fresh. He'd never eaten fresh vegetables and had to ask what each one was.

As soon as he finished eating, he could hardly keep his eyes open. Trying not to be ungrateful, he excused himself and went to the bedroom he'd been assigned. He was just preparing for bed when he heard Ma and Pops arguing in the kitchen.

"Are you going to send that boy off to Ernst and his bunch?"

"Where else should we send him? Without an education, what can he do other than ranch work? At least they'll take care of him and he won't have to work his ass off doing manual labor. Who knows, maybe Ernst is right about what is going on in this country. If I don't miss my guess, Christopher has a fine mind. If he finds this isn't something he wants, he'll at least have a chance to make his own decision, and he might even find someone who can help him more than we can. For now, he's another of the young men we've picked up over the years. Besides, it does help us out in more ways than one."

Until recently, Christopher had never thought much about not having an education, but listening to Pops and Ma, he was suddenly ashamed of what he didn't know. He had no idea what he was getting into, but maybe the group headed by Patrick Ernst would be the best place for him.

~ * ~

Three days after leaving Henderson Ranch, Christopher had a visitor. The young man identified himself as Patrick Ernst.

"Pops told me you want to join us," Patrick said, after the initial introductions were made.

"I guess so. I don't have anywhere else to go. My friend, Marco, told me about your group. He thought I might fit in quite well."

"What do you know about our mission?"

Christopher thought for a moment before answering. "Just that you are the leader of men my age."

"I wouldn't call you a man. What are you, eighteen?"

Christopher nodded. "I aged out of the system at Henderson

Ranch three days ago. They told me I'm eighteen now and I had to leave."

"What can you do?"

"Ranching and carpentry. I can write my name but little else. I have been told I can learn anything you want me to know."

"What about your folks? Why did they send you to Henderson?"

"I don't have any folks. The story I heard is my father was killed in a hover craft crash and my mother died from her injuries right after I was born. I wasn't supposed to live, but when I did, they sent me to Henderson. I've lived there all my life."

Patrick smiled at Christopher's admission. "Sounds like you'll fit right in. That said, we have to get going. I want to be back to camp by nightfall."

To Christopher's surprise, Patrick ran his fingers through his thick hair. "I'm afraid this will have to go."

Christopher knew what was coming next. Patrick's head was shaved bald. For a moment, indecision fought to take over Christopher's being.

Swallowing down his doubt, he said, "Why not? It's just hair, it will grow back."

"Not as long as you're with us. We're not called skinheads for nothing."

Within minutes, Ma's kitchen was turned into a makeshift barber shop. Using power clippers, Patrick cut through Christopher's dark hair. Seeing it drop to the floor brought a feeling of loss followed by anticipation for what was to come.

Once the lengths of hair were on the floor, Patrick took him to the bathroom. Using shaving cream on the top of his head, he showed Christopher how to shave his head on a weekly basis.

From the mirror positioned over the sink, he stared at the stranger who looked back. *Am I ready for this?*

"It's a shock when you first see it, but you'll get used to it. I have some fatigues for you to put on. This is going to be your uniform from now on."

Christopher fingered the soft fabric of the fatigues. They look like they would be much more comfortable than the blue jeans he'd worn all his life. He went into his bedroom, not because he was modest, but because he respected Ma enough not to strip down in her presence.

The fatigues hugged his body and made him feel like a different person. He was no longer the scared kid who left Henderson Ranch. For the first time in his life, he was a man who belonged to a group of other young men like himself.

After saying his good-byes to Pops and Ma, he joined Patrick in his hover craft to begin the biggest adventure of his life.

They were on their way to Idaho when Christopher remembered the money that he'd put in the top dresser drawer when he first arrived. "I didn't get the money Mrs. Henderson gave me. We have to go back and get it."

"Don't worry about it, you won't need it while you're with us. If it makes you feel any better, I'll contact Pops and have Ma look for it. She can send it to you at our camp."

Christopher relaxed and decided to enjoy the ride on the hover craft. Having never been in one before, he decided it was many times better than riding horseback on the ranch for hours on end each day.

Chapter Three

Within a week, Christopher felt as though he'd found his home. He attended classes where he was indoctrinated into the ideology of Patrick's group.

He soon learned about how the people of color were planning to take over the world, the government was corrupt and the Aliens who came to this planet were planning the destruction of the human race.

It didn't take him long to learn how to use a laser weapon. He was surprised at how quickly he mastered the use of his weapon.

While many of the new recruits were quickly assessed and eventually asked to leave as they didn't have the guts for what the group was proposing to do, Christopher thrived. He quickly rose through the ranks to become Patrick's second in command. He embraced the ideals and resolved to fight for what was right until the end. If he died for his beliefs, so be it.

For the first two years he'd been with the group, he saw no action, as Patrick called it. They spent hours practicing for the day when they would be called upon to protest against the establishment.

~ * ~

2120

"Did you see these headlines?" Patrick asked when he came into the barracks.

"What headlines?"

"It seems like the Aliens have finally done it. They've brought a woman back to life from Suspended Animation. They think she's going to be the next National Treasure. They've got to be stopped. She's telling

14

lies about what happened in the past. She has to be exposed as a hoax. Tomorrow we leave for Colorado and the headquarters of the Aliens. With luck we can get into their complex and kick a lot of ass. Hopefully we can kill us a bunch of Aliens. I wonder if they bleed red like us or if they bleed green. I heard my old man call them little green men."

"I don't know nothing about Aliens but this could be interesting," Christopher agreed.

Inside, his stomach was in knots. So far, he'd enjoyed the training and the friends he'd made within the organization. Training was one thing, putting what he'd learned into practice was something else.

Early the next morning, they loaded their hover crafts with weapons, provisions, and a hundred of the highest trained soldiers in their ranks and left for Colorado.

Having spent his entire life living in a country setting, Christopher was unprepared for the congestion of the city where the Alien's complex was located.

"Do we have a chance of penetrating that?" Christopher asked.

"Our weapons can penetrate anything," Patrick assured him. "We have to stop this bitch from talking about history. It's all a bunch of fuckin' shit as far as I'm concerned. A lot of things they're talking about are nothing but crap. What I learned in school is enough for me. I don't give a rat's ass about ancient history, and that's just what they're preaching."

As they approached the complex, they watched as a protective shield came down around the entire area.

Patrick was the first to aim his weapon at the shield. To Christopher's horror, the laser beam bounded off the shield. For the first time, he wished he hadn't aligned himself with this group. It was entirely possible he could be killed in the battle that was to come. If he wasn't killed, he could be captured and executed for treason. Even without a formal education, he'd heard enough about treason from some of the recruits who left the group to be fearful.

They camped for the night, ready for the assault that would take place early the next morning.

Drones equipped with cameras flew over the next morning. "Let's have some fun," Patrick said, jabbing Christopher in his ribs. "Watch this."

Patrick looked directly at the camera, pumped his fist into the air and yelled, "History doesn't matter!"

He no more than spoke the words when well-armed military troops infiltrated the area where they camped.

"Put down your arms," someone called through a blowhorn. "You're surrounded, there's no way for you to escape."

To Christopher's horror, two of the younger recruits fired their weapons. The military returned fire, killing both of the young men instantly. It took only a moment for Christopher to realize the two men who were killed were two of his friends. They'd been in the last training class Christopher led while they were still in Idaho.

Not wanting to look unmanly, he choked back the tears that threatened to fall at any minute. Reluctantly, they laid down their arms.

"What's going to happen to us?" Christopher whispered to Patrick.

"How the fuck should I know? It wasn't supposed to go like this."

"Who are the leaders of this group?" the man on the blowhorn shouted.

Following Patrick's lead, Christopher stepped forward. "We are," Christopher said when Patrick stood mute.

"We're from the National Guard. It's too bad about the two men you lost. We wanted this to be peaceful. The governor and the president have asked for a meeting between you and them in the morning. Do you agree to this?"

"We do," Christopher said as Patrick seemed to tremble with fear.

"For tonight you are to stand down and shelter in place. In the morning, you will be taken into the complex by one of our guards."

Christopher could feel Patrick's fear. It was the same fear he'd felt upon leaving Henderson Ranch, the fear of the unknown. He'd heard all the rumors about what went on within the Alien complex. Would they become lab rats? If not, would they be murdered and eaten? Whatever happened, he would accept it. He was fighting for what was right and if it cost him his life, so be it.

"I feel downright naked without my weapon," one of the men complained. "It's wrong for us to be left out here defenseless."

"You saw what happened to Tim and Joe. Do you want the troops to shoot you down like a dog?" The reply came from another of the nameless recruits that made up their number.

Christopher made no comment. It was beginning to look like theirs was a lost cause. With the National Guard and threats of federal troops coming to subdue them, they were completely outnumbered both in personnel and fire power.

~ * ~

Early the next morning, armed guards from the complex came out to their camp. Amid their preparations for departure, there were comments both pro and con regarding this meeting.

Christopher felt the bile of uncertainty raising in his throat. Swallowing it down, he held his head high. If this was going to be his last day on Earth, he wanted no one to think he was a coward.

The room where they were taken was filled with cameras, as well as people in all modes of dress. Among them were two older men dressed in suits, an older woman who was the most beautiful woman he'd ever seen, and several people he decided were Aliens. They were much taller than all the others and had an exotic look about them.

"I'm President Brian Addison. I'd like to welcome you to this meeting."

The man held out his hand, but Patrick ignored it. "We are here at the request of the government and the Aliens," Patrick said, a sneer in his voice. "We are against all of this ancient history crap. We are also against the Aliens coming to take over our country. We recognize only the superior race."

"Hogwash," the older woman shouted. "This superior race you're talking about was a product of the mind of a sick individual named

Adolph Hitler."

Patrick's expression changed from one of hatred to one of bewilderment. "Who are you talking about?"

Christopher shared in Patrick's bewilderment, whilst the woman continued.

"I'm talking about the man who first decided people who weren't white, blonde and blue eyed weren't worth living. I have a feeling, by looking at your beards, you aren't blondes and neither of you have blue eyes. Had you lived in Hitler's Germany, you might have been sent to a concentration camp, starved and possibly sent to the gas chamber. You are blessed to be able to live in a country where you are free to voice your opinion. The problem, as I see it, is with history and the monuments depicting it being eradicated, you have no idea what happened before you or even your parents were born. I suggest you, as well as your associates, take the time to read the bits and pieces of history that I have been able to fill in. I realize it's not complete by any stretch of the imagination, but once you know what price was paid for your freedom, you might understand what we are hoping to bring back to the people of Earth."

"Are you certain about this?" Patrick questioned.

The woman seemed to relax as she answered Patrick's question. "I'm positive. Violence cures nothing whatsoever. How many of your people have you lost because of the violence you are perpetuating?"

Christopher could no longer hold back his tears. "I lost my two of my friends. I thought it was because of the government and I wanted to fight them. Now I can see that I was wrong. Can you teach me about this history I haven't learned?"

The woman held out her hand to him. "I feel so sorry for the people of this generation who know nothing of history. I can fill in some of the gaps, but until a program of teaching what has been lost is instituted, it won't be complete. What you do need to know is that the Aliens have come here to advise, rather than to rule. I have toured their home base under the ice cap of Antarctica and was extremely impressed. We have much to learn from these people, but first and foremost we much learn from the past."

"I heard you talk of race riots," Patrick said. "What were they?"

"Let me answer this one," the older man replied. "Since I've met my wife, I've done extensive research. In the early days of our country, black people were kidnapped from their homes in Africa and brought here as slaves. Even when they were freed, they were still looked upon as second class citizens. For many years it was white versus black. Over history other people have been discriminated against. Be they Irish, German, Oriental, Hispanic, black, white, red or yellow, we are all created equal. Even the Native Americans who were here before any of the other settlers arrived were persecuted and many of them were wiped out. There is no superior race, just narrow-minded prejudice."

The words Native American resonated within the confines of Christopher's mind. For all of his life, he had been told because he had Native American blood, even though his skin was pale, was the reason he'd been sent to the Henderson Ranch. No one wanted to adopt a child with mixed blood. He was an abomination whom no one wanted. Only Pops, Ma and Patrick accepted him for what he was rather than who he was.

The noon meal was served, and Christopher found himself seated next to the older woman who told him her name was Caroline.

"How do you know so much about this ancient history stuff?" he asked, once their meal was served.

Caroline broke into a wide grin. "Over a hundred years ago there was a terrible disease taking over the world. My husband was away on a business trip when he contracted it and died. I didn't want to go on without him, so I decided to put my body into a state of suspended animation. I was planning to be awakened in fifty years, but there were many disasters that delayed the process for another fifty years. I know much of what I speak because it happened either in my lifetime or the lifetimes of my parents and grandparents. I also studied world history in college. My memory never dimmed during the time I was asleep."

Christopher had no idea about some of the things she was saying. He'd never had parents or grandparents in his life. As for college, he had no idea what it was, but something within him wanted to know.

"Do you think we could meet privately, away from all the others? I want to know more, but I don't want Patrick to…"

"To what?"

"I don't know, but I have a feeling in my gut there are things you can tell me that Patrick wouldn't understand."

"If that's the case, of course I'll meet with you privately. I would enjoy hearing about your life."

~ * ~

While Patrick and the others remained in the conference room, a security officer led Caroline and Christopher into a private meeting room.

"Thank you for agreeing to meet with me privately," he said once they were seated on two of the overstuffed chairs. "I have some questions and I didn't want to ask them in front of Patrick."

"I can understand your need for privacy. What is it you want to know?"

Christopher ran his hand over his shaved head. He remembered having a full head of dark brown hair. When the Henderson's refused to cut it, he sometimes pulled it back and secured it with a piece of cloth torn from the cleaning rags that were given to the boys in order for them to clean their living quarters. For the past two years, he'd shaved his head on a regular basis, but at the same time he missed his hair.

"I don't know anything about my family. I was brought up in an orphanage, because both of my parents were killed in a hover craft accident on their way to, I don't know where. My father was killed instantly and my mother lived long enough for the doctors to deliver me by Caesarian section. They didn't have any identification, so the authorities didn't know who to call. When I was strong enough to make the trip, I was taken to an orphanage. I was told because my DNA showed I was Native American, it was impossible for them to place me for adoption. I never knew what that meant and no one at the orphanage could tell me anything about it.

"Don't get me wrong, I had a good upbringing at the orphanage. I learned how to work hard, but I wanted to know what it was like to have a family. When I turned eighteen, I aged out of the program and I met up with Patrick and the others. For the first time I had people who cared about me because I was me. No one knew about the stigma that kept me from being adopted. I was ashamed of it, more because I had no idea what it meant than for who I was."

He regretted the white lie he'd told about his life in the orphanage. It was too painful to recall the poor meals, hard work and harsh punishments he endured during the first eighteen years of his life.

"I heard your husband mention atrocities done against the Native Americans, but who were they?"

Caroline wiped tears from her eyes. It hurt him to see this woman so sad at what he said.

"I guess I should start at the beginning. First, I would like to know if your DNA denoted the identity of the tribe you're associated with."

Christopher reached into the pocket of his pants and pulled out the paper Mrs. Henderson gave him on the day he was released from their care. "This is what I was given when I left the orphanage, but I didn't know what any of it meant."

"Are you telling me you don't know how to read?"

Christopher shook his head. "I was told I was a nobody. My name was given to me by the doctor who treated my mother. I was told I was so premature they didn't think I would survive the night after I was born. I guess I beat the odds. At the orphanage, education was not a top priority. I know enough to sign my name and add two and two, but that's about it. Those of us who were deemed unadoptable were taught a trade. My trade was a carpenter as well as being able to work on a ranch. Of course, there wasn't much call for someone like me when I aged out. I also know ranching, but I never enjoyed it. I was lucky to find Patrick and the others."

Christopher watched as Caroline scanned the paper that he'd given her. "It says here you have European ancestry as well as Cheyenne heritage. The Cheyenne, along with the other tribes that populated this country before the white man came to take their land as well as their lives, have been treated terribly. When I did my Native American studies, the Cheyenne were the ones who were the most interesting to me. If you would like to learn more about them, I would be honored to teach you not only about your ancestors but also how to read and write. Of course, that would mean you would have to leave Patrick's group and come to live here at the complex. I know there are many others here who would be excellent teachers for you."

Worry and concern filled his mind. "I don't know how Patrick and the others would feel about me leaving them to come to live here."

"Why don't we just sit quietly for a while and pray on it?" Caroline suggested.

"Pray? What is that?"

With that one question, Caroline broke down in tears. He had no idea why she was shedding such heart wrenching tears and sobbing as though she was in pain.

"I think you need more guidance than I'm equipped to give you. There is a woman here who can be of great help to you. Her name is Hodia and she is very knowledgeable about God and prayer."

Christopher was confused. Wasn't god one of the swear words Mr. Henderson and the members of Patrick's group enjoyed using so freely. Could it be there was another meaning? One which he had no idea what it was.

He watched in amazement as Caroline tapped on the device on her wrist. He'd seen Mr. and Mrs. Henderson doing the same thing with similar devices, but he didn't know what they were used for. Usually if Mrs. Henderson tapped on it, Mr. Henderson appeared at the house to punish him for some unknown reason.

Hodia arrived within minutes of Caroline tapping on the device. Christopher knew he should get up out of respect for the woman, but his legs seemed to have turned to jelly and his body seemed to be too heavy to lift out of the chair.

"I'm Hodia," she said as she entered the room. "I'm told you are Christopher."

He looked up, for some reason his earlier tears were again stinging in his eyes. "You're one of the Aliens who want to take over our planet, aren't you?"

"I am an Alien, as you call me, but neither I, nor any of my comrades, want to take over your planet. We are merely advisors, trying to right some of the wrongs that have been done here over the centuries."

"Ms. Lewis-Phillips wants me to stay here to be educated. I don't know what to do. You aren't going to use me for medical research, are you? That's what Patrick says you do here."

"Patrick is mistaken. We don't do that kind of research here or at any of our other bases. Our research is done to perfect vaccines and medications to heal the illnesses of all the humans on this planet. I'm confused, you're very well spoken, but you mentioned being in need of education."

Once again, Christopher related the story of his birth and upbringing in the orphanage. Like Caroline, Hodia was moved to tears.

"I never thought I would hear of such a horror story in this day and age. I studied some of the histories of the orphanages, work houses and the like in the eighteenth and nineteenth centuries, but I never thought I would hear about such things in modern times. This will have to be investigated and those responsible will be dealt with. I agree with Caroline, I would be honored to have you come to live at the complex and allow us to see to your education. From what I can tell, you have a fine mind. Perhaps you can become a link between us and the militants. The way I see it, education and knowledge of the past are going to be very important in the future of Earth."

All his life, he'd been told he was inadequate. How could these people offer him what he'd been denied? There was a hint of something different in their voices. In a way they reminded him of Ma. She was the only person who used the word love in conjunction with him. He remembered her holding him tight and whispering that he was loved in his ear, when he was ready to walk out of their lives to go with Patrick. Was it possible the strange feeling was love? He didn't know but he wanted to find out.

"I-I would like to have an education. Can I see Patrick and tell him of these plans before he leaves?"

Hodia nodded and held out her hand. Without hesitation, he took it, like a lost child who was learning to respect and trust adults.

Outside the door, the security guard waited for them to exit the room. Hodia dismissed him with nothing more than a wave of her hand and the three of them made their way back to the conference room.

~ * ~

Patrick didn't want to show it, but he was worried when Christopher asked for a private meeting with the older woman who yelled at them earlier. Even with a security guard going with them, once they were in the private office, anything could happen.

"Why did Christopher want to talk to that bitch alone?" Patrick spat.

He knew his words were laced with anger.

"I have no idea but you will not use such vulgar language in reference to my wife. I'd like for you to answer a question for me."

"Why should I, old man?"

"Because this man has done nothing to harm you," one of the aliens who had been introduced as Dr. Gratan responded. "To be truthful, no one here has done you harm. We are all interested in a peaceful end to this protest. What is it that has made you so angry?"

Patrick hesitated for a moment, thoughtfully considering his answer. "All this talk about history is ridiculous. I went to school and I never heard anything about what that lady was saying. I have no idea who this Adolph Hitler was and I don't need to know. Our group is as old as time itself. My parents taught me about the inferiority of all the races but our own. Now you want to bring up ancient history and it makes no sense."

"Your education, like that of most of Earth's population, is lacking when it comes to the history Ms. Lewis-Phillips has brought to light," President Addison said. "I have done a lot of research into the history of this country and I admit I knew next to nothing about these things. I'm

24

willing to learn from the mistakes of the past. Would you be willing to call off this protest and weigh all of your options?"

Before Patrick could answer, the door to the conference room opened. He turned to see Caroline, Christopher and an alien woman enter the room.

He stared at Christopher and could see something had changed as far as his second in command was concerned.

"I was afraid you wouldn't come back, Buddy," Patrick said, grasping Christopher's forearm. "What did they do to you?"

"They didn't do anything. They offered to give me the education I was denied and the chance to learn about my heritage. You've been good to me, but I think I want more out of life. What you don't know is that my DNA says I have Native American blood. With that, I can't be a member of your group. I should have told you this in the beginning, but I had no idea what it meant."

The wind went out of Patrick's sails. "Do you mean to tell me there might be something to this history crap?"

"There is," President Addison replied. "Since you're the leader of these people, would you agree to work with us? By us, I mean, everyone in this complex as well as the military and myself, to bring this to a peaceful end."

The room became suddenly silent. Everyone looked to Patrick, anxious to know what his answer would be.

Thoughts of imprisonment, torture and possibly death ran through his mind like a runaway storm. "Will we be under arrest?" he asked, almost afraid to hear the answer.

"I give you my word, if you will work with us, there will be no charges brought against any of you. The one condition is that you must turn in your weapons. Is that something you can agree to?"

Slowly Patrick nodded his head in agreement. "I'm man enough to take you at your word. Maybe this history thing might be good for our country."

He turned toward Christopher. "Are you sure you want to stay here, man?"

"I'm sure. You've been good to me, but I need to know who I am. It's possible I have people like me who will accept me. These people aren't our enemies. They want to help all of the people of Earth. I'm not the smartest person in our group, but I want to learn everything I've been denied in the past."

Again, Patrick grasped Christopher's forearm. "You're a good man. If you think this is a good move, I tend to agree with you. President Addison has said there will be no charges brought against any of us. It's entirely possible the time for protests and war is over."

Patrick prepared to leave the conference room. He'd spoken the words he knew they expected him to speak in order for them to let him go. Only time would tell what he would do with the rest of his life. What he did know was that he'd misjudged Christopher. The little bastard wasn't pure white. It was possible he'd always known about his Native American blood and hid that information from the rest of the group. He certainly wouldn't make the mistake of taking in someone without checking their DNA chip again.

Chapter Four

Christopher knew he should go outside and say good-bye to the members of the group he'd been with for the past two years, but for some reason he hung back. From everything he'd learned from his comrades, their knowledge of his Native American blood would make him an outcast. They, like the people who raised him, and those who wouldn't adopt him, would think less of him and he couldn't stand the feeling of being rejected once again.

If he could believe Hodia and Caroline, he should be proud of his heritage and learn everything he could about the ancestors he knew nothing about.

"Don't you want to say good-bye to your friends," a young woman who was about his age asked.

Christopher shook his head. "I have no friends," he said sadly. "The only one of them I was close to was Patrick and I told him I was leaving, that's enough. The only others were the two who were killed last night. I trained them and thought of them as friends. Of course, they're gone and won't be coming back."

He noticed a look of concern on the woman's face. She was definitely one of the aliens but she was lovely.

"You'll make friends here. My name is Melian. My aunt sent me to take you to the apartment we have set aside for you. If you let me, I'd like to be your friend."

"I'd like that. Did you say apartment? Not just a room?"

"I did say an apartment. Now, you're supposed to follow me. I've been sent here to make certain you're comfortable. Once you see where you're going to be living, I'm to bring you to my aunt's office. She wants to get you something other than *that* to wear and see what you'll need for your education."

For the first time in two years, he was ashamed of the clothes he had been wearing. He longed for the jeans, boots and shirts he'd left behind at Pops and Ma's place.

"I didn't think my clothes were so offensive."

"Don't get me wrong. They are just different from what everyone here wears. They also don't smell the greatest."

Christopher laughed at her statement. "I'm sure they don't smell like sweet flowers. I've been wearing them for the last three days. Usually don't go that long without changing clothes, but these are the only ones I have. I don't think I would be welcome with the group that follows Patrick. Even if I were, we didn't have room to bring much with us."

"I like you. If I'm lucky, Aunt Zora will let me help you with your studies. I want to be a teacher. To be truthful, I didn't want to come here in the first place, but my parents thought it was for the best."

Christopher took a long hard look at Melian. Was it possible she was more like him than he first thought? Was she living at the complex with her aunt because her own parents didn't want her?

He could tell she was becoming impatient with him. He urged her to lead the way into the unknown of the complex. Together they made their way to a bank of elevators. Even though they were like nothing he'd ever seen before, he decided she must know what she was doing. "That looks like the smallest room I've ever seen," he commented.

"This isn't your apartment, silly. This is an elevator. It will take us up to the floor where your apartment is located."

"How will it do that?"

"Don't you know what an elevator is?"

"Never saw one before in my life. There was no need for one on the ranch where I grew up and at the camp if we wanted to go upstairs, we walked up the steps."

"I have a feeling, getting to know you and helping you with your education is going to be the most fun I've had since I came here."

Reluctantly, Christopher followed Melian into the small cubical. When the door closed and the room began to move, he started to panic. Was this a trap? Beside the door was a panel, on it he saw numbers start to go up. He knew enough to know they went to the upper levels of the complex. He remembered thinking it was the tallest thing he'd ever seen. Even the trees at the camp in Idaho that reached so far up into the sky weren't this tall.

He was hardly aware of the movement of the room when it stopped. The pad next to the door read fifteen. Since Melian seemed to be pleased, he watched as the door opened. Unlike the floor where he'd been for most of the day, this one had a long hallway.

Melian exited the room and walked purposely down to a door with the number fifteen twenty-six on it. She pressed her hand against the recognition pad beside the door and it slid open as silently as the one on the elevator. She stepped inside and motioned for Christopher to follow her.

Once inside the apartment, Christopher looked around. He'd never seen anything so elegant in his entire life. Everything was clean and modern. "This-this can't be for me."

"Yes, it can. Of course, this is a bachelor apartment. You see, there isn't a kitchen. Meals are served in the dining room on the first floor. This is the living room and the room over there is the bedroom." She stepped across the room and opened another door with the wave of her hand.

With the door open, he saw the biggest bed he'd ever seen before in his entire life. "Who else lives here?"

"No one, silly. This is your apartment. The last tenant was here with a delegation from the dark side of the moon, and his assignment was up. Everything has been cleaned and redecorated. Is it not to your liking?"

"I like it very much, but I've never lived anywhere like this before. To be, to be truthful, I've never slept in a room without a lot of other guys. I take that back, when I first left the ranch, Pops and Ma let me sleep in their spare bedroom. I wasn't there long enough to know if I liked sleeping by myself or not."

"You'll get used to it. Now that you know where you will be living, I have to get you down to Aunt Zora's office. She'll set it up so you can use your palm print to open the door and contact the proper people to get you a new wardrobe."

"I don't have any money. Patrick says everyone needs money. I had a hundred dollars when I left the ranch, but when I left Pops and Ma's place, I didn't have it. I guess it paid for everything I needed when I was with them. Patrick told me Ma would probably send it to me, but it never arrived."

Melian rolled her eyes as though she didn't believe a word he said. He made no mention of his assumptions and followed her back to the elevator. He committed the pathway through the hallway to memory, so he would be able to come back there later in the day.

Even though the elevator still terrified him, Christopher put his fears to rest as he stepped into the cubical for the ride back down to the first floor where Melian told him her aunt's office was located.

~ * ~

Zora, Caroline, Hodia, Cassion, Aaron and President Addison gathered in Zora's office to discuss the plans for Christopher's reeducation.

"What's your take on this young man, Caroline?" Zora asked.

"I think he's highly intelligent, but he's never had a chance at a proper education. He says he can write his name and do simple math, but that's about it. Why, he didn't even know anything about God. I was horrified."

"I've done some checking on that ranch he said he grew up on," Hodia said. "From what I could find, it's located in a very remote area of Nevada. The pictures on the internet make it sound like a paradise. The state pays them to take in and raise orphans who are exempt from adoption for one reason or another. According to the hype on their website, the boys they take in are well educated and given a good Christian upbringing. It certainly doesn't fit the description of the place Christopher gave us."

"You can say anything on the Internet, we've known that for over a hundred and twenty years," President Addison added. "I think it's about time someone investigates this ranch."

"Why hasn't someone reported it before this?" Caroline asked.

"If all the kids are as uneducated as Christopher, it's possible they don't know any better. The lack of education leaves them thinking the only thing they are good for is manual labor. It will be hard to track them all down. If I don't miss my guess most of them have gone to ranches in Mexico. Ranching seems to be something they taught those boys."

"I think you're right, Brian," Caroline said. "He mentioned one of his friends was of Mexican descent. What are the rules on bi-racial adoptions in this country?"

"You must know there aren't a lot of adoptions anymore. Christopher said something about being Native American, was that in his DNA?"

"The papers they gave him when he left the ranch by Mrs. Henderson said so. He had no idea what they said, but from what I gathered, he has Native American blood, Cheyenne to be exact, as well as European. He also told me his father was killed in a hover craft accident and his mother died shortly after giving birth to him. Among those papers were ones saying where he was born and the name of the doctor who treated the mother. I think that would be a good place to start. Someone, somewhere, must be looking for him. We'll know more once we are able to do a complete scan of his DNA chip."

A knock at the door ended the discussion.

"Enter," Zora said.

Everyone looked toward the door and saw Melian and Christopher enter.

~ * ~

"Are your accommodations satisfactory?" Zora asked.

"It's more than I expected, Ma'am. I can't believe the whole thing is for me."

"You deserve it. We wanted to talk to you for a little while before you go to pick out new clothes and get your handprint registered so you can gain entry to your apartment."

Christopher nodded. "That's what Miss Melian told me. I ain't ever bought new clothes before. I don't know how to do it."

"Cassion and I will be more than happy to help you with your selections," Aaron said. "You'll get the hang of things and will probably turn into a shopaholic."

He had no idea what Aaron meant, but he didn't want to appear to be too ignorant in the ways of the world.

"Christopher said he's worried about the fact he doesn't have any money," Melian commented. "I told him that, for now, he wouldn't have to worry about that. I wasn't wrong to tell him that, was I Aunt Zora?"

"You were correct."

Christopher let out a sigh of relief.

Zora turned her attention from her niece to him. "While you are here, you are a student and your needs will be taken care of, including food, clothing, education and spending money. What we expect from you is your cooperation and a willingness to learn everything we have to teach you."

"I am anxious to learn everything I can. I hope I'm not too old or too stupid to learn."

"Whoever told you anything like that?" Hodia asked, getting to her feet. "No one is ever too old to learn and you are far from stupid. I'm outraged to think anyone would ever tell you such a thing. We intend to investigate Henderson Ranch and rescue as many of the children we possibly can."

The things these people were saying were beyond his comprehension. No one cared for the unadoptable children at the ranch in the past. Why were these people so concerned about kids they didn't know?

"Since you are of age," President Addison said, "do we have your permission to look into your DNA and try to find your family?"

"You can try, but from what I'm told, I have no family anywhere. That's the reason I was sent to the ranch in the first place."

"Were you happy there?" Hodia asked, her voice now softer than it was before.

"I don't know how to answer that. I honestly don't have any idea what happy means. I was given something to eat in the morning and again at night. I worked either in the carpentry shop or on the ranch from the time I finished eating the morning meal until dark when the night meal was served."

"What about schooling?" President Addison pressed.

"Like I told Caroline, they taught us just what was necessary. I learned enough numbers so I could work in the carpentry shop. Otherwise, the only thing I was taught was how to write my name. Mrs. Henderson said that undesirables like me didn't need to know anything else."

He was surprised to see the women in the room openly crying. He'd cried earlier in the day, but it was the first time in years. The last time he remembered crying, he was ten years old and had been thrown off a horse that got spooked and tried to jump a fence to get away from a snake. When Mr. Henderson picked him up from the ground, he was given a whipping for crying. That was the last time he'd shed tears in front of anyone.

"We won't start your classes until the beginning of next week," Zora announced. "Since it's Thursday, you can take tomorrow and Saturday to rest. On Sunday, you're more than welcome to join us at church. It's high time you learned about the One God and why we worship him."

He wasn't too sure about the God thing. Until he came here, he never even heard about God, Christianity or church. He didn't know what any of it meant or if it was anything he could embrace. He decided it would do him no good to do anything to make these people not want to help him with an education and perhaps a family.

Chapter Five

The weekend seemed to fly by. Christopher was given a new wardrobe, which was delivered to his apartment. Living by himself was the hardest thing for him to get used to. When he retired to his apartment for the night, he found he was lonely. He missed the other men and boys he'd lived with all his life. He also missed living mostly outdoors.

At the ranch, they'd all slept in the bunkhouse but only went there at night when they were no longer needed for outside work. It was the same at the camp with Patrick's group. The barracks were not used during the day, since everyone was outside training.

Thinking about the camp, he remembered Pops telling him he would get three hots' and a cot there. At the time he had no idea what the old man was talking about. In his entire life there had never been more than two meals a day. At the camp he enjoyed eating breakfast, lunch and supper. It might not always be hot, but it was food to fuel his body. He soon equated his bunk with the cot Pops talked about. The living conditions weren't ideal but they were a step up from life on the ranch.

The life he was now becoming accustomed to was luxurious beyond belief. Cassion told him his room would be cleaned and his clothes laundered for him as part of his life as a student. He was also instructed to change into fresh clothing every day. It was a far cry from how he'd lived before.

On the ranch, he had two sets of clothing. No matter how dirty they got, he was allowed to bathe only once a week and at that time he could change his clothes. It was the same at the camp. Cleanliness wasn't anything that was promoted.

He had to admit he liked being clean and having access to a shower in his apartment on a daily basis.

This morning, I'm going to begin my education. I hope I am up to the task.

A knock at the door interrupted his inner thoughts. Before he could get to his feet to answer it, the computerized identification system announced, *Melian is waiting for permission to enter your apartment.*

He hurried to the door and swiped his hand across the identification pad, signaling the door to slide open.

"Are you ready for your first day of school?" Melian asked.

The words seemed to bubble out of her mouth as she entered his apartment. He liked the way she was always so excited about whatever they were going to be doing for the day. He could never remember being excited about anything.

"Should I be?" he asked.

"Of course, you should. Aunt Zora has a classroom set up for you and a lot of teachers who are anxious to work with you."

"Will you be one of my teachers?" he asked, surprising himself by being so forward with this young woman.

He had absolutely no experience with the opposite sex. He heard the men at the camp talking about women, but they were all very derogatory in their remarks. He'd never thought of Mrs. Henderson as a sexual person, and Ma was more the motherly type than someone he would be attracted to. He made a mental note to ask one of the men about this if they were among his teachers.

Thinking about Henderson Ranch, he remembered Mr. Henderson telling them about the facts of life. "All women are whores. That's why most of you are here. Your mothers were whores and they had no idea who your fathers were. Why else would they abandon you the way they did? They couldn't ply their trade with a screaming brat clinging to their skirts."

He knew his situation was different because his mother died shortly after his birth. At least that's what Mrs. Henderson told him. What if she hadn't died? Was she out there, plying her trade, as Mr. Henderson said? Was there really a father who was killed, or was he someone who was made up for convenience?

"Earth to Christopher," Melian said, waving her hand in front of his face. "Are you with me or somewhere else?"

"I'm sorry, I was thinking about the past. I shouldn't do that. Today is going to be a new beginning for me. I don't think I want to be Christopher anymore."

"Why not?"

"Christopher was an ignorant child who no one wanted. I need more in my life than that. From now on I will be Chris. Do you think the others will understand?"

"Of course, they will. Christopher is too long a name to use all the time. I think Chris is a perfect name for you."

She threw her arms around his neck and he felt strange sensations in an area of his body where he'd never felt them before. *This is something else I need to ask someone about.*

~ * ~

Zora and Caroline went over the schedule for Christopher's schooling.

"This is an awful lot of classes and information," Caroline lamented. "Do you think it will be overwhelming to him?"

"You said you thought he had a brilliant mind. I think you're right. I have a feeling he will learn the rudiments of reading, writing and math rather quickly. That's why this accelerated program is so important. If I'm right, he will be ready for higher studies within a very short period of time. We have to remember he's a man, and one who is eager to learn. Did you see him in church yesterday? He was absorbing everything the pastor said like a sponge. It will be the same with his education."

Their conversation was interrupted when Melian and Christopher entered the room. Seeing him dressed in pants and a shirt, with athletic shoes replacing the boots he'd worn when they first met him made them smile in amazement. Dark fuzz that would soon become hair were sporting on his head while his beard had been shaved.

"Good morning, Caroline, Zora. I guess I'm ready to begin my education. I do have one request, though. From now on, Christopher is dead. I've made the decision to change my name to Chris. I'm a man who is looking for an education. Christopher was an unwanted child. He has to be gone forever."

Caroline smiled at his proclamation. "That is a very adult decision. I think I can speak for all of us when I say you are making us very proud."

~ * ~

By the time for the noon meal came, Chris thought he'd learned so much more than he ever thought possible. Letters he'd learned as a child were suddenly becoming words and words were becoming sentences. A whole new world was opening up to him and he wanted to learn more and more.

When Melian came to go to lunch with him, he was reluctant to leave the classroom. "What if I miss something? There is so much to learn, I don't want to waste a minute by going to get something to eat."

"Now you're being silly," she chided. "We all need to eat. You'll have plenty of time for learning after you fuel your body as well as your mind."

Reluctantly, he closed the book he'd been reading. Even though he knew it was the most elementary of the readers, he was anxious to learn more and more.

At the dining room, they were met by Cassion. For some unknown reason, the look that Cassion gave Melian caused her to excuse herself from their presence.

"How do you think your first classes went?" Cassion asked when he took a seat opposite Chris.

"I never knew what I was missing. I'm learning to read and it's the most rewarding thing I've ever done in my life. How long do you think it will be before I can read anything I want, without struggling over the words?"

"At the rate you're going, it shouldn't be long. This afternoon I will be your teacher. You need to know more than two plus two equals four. If you take to that like you have to reading, the student could easily surpass the teacher."

Chris laughed. "I doubt that. There is so much I don't know, but I want to learn."

"That's what I wanted to hear. Speaking of hearing things, I was told you want to shorten your name. I think you've made a good decision. Even though you haven't been here for very long, I can see you aren't the same man who came to us last week. Is there anything else I can help you with?"

Chris thought for a long moment. "I'm having feelings I don't understand. All my life I've been told women are whores, but when I'm with Melian I don't think that way. She makes me feel funny in areas I never have before. What's wrong with me?"

"Nothing is wrong with you, Chris. You're a normal twenty-year-old man. You're feeling attraction to someone of the opposite sex. While our society doesn't condone sexual relations between a man and a woman before marriage, we know not everyone shares our views. I would hope you will embrace our values, but the choice is yours to make."

Chris liked the way Cassion put things. He wished he would have had a father like this man who was talking to him as though he was an equal. He knew there was nothing he couldn't talk to him about.

Once they finished eating their lunch, they returned to the classroom. Starting with basic math, it was amazing how quickly Chris was able to master basic addition and subtraction. As soon as the numbers were presented to him, he was eager to take the next step.

"I think we've done enough for today," Cassion announced.

"There has to be more. I want to keep going," Chris protested.

"I know you do, but it has been a long afternoon. We both need to rest so we can continue tomorrow. I know there will be more reading lessons and I need to prepare some higher mathematical problems for you. You have an amazing mind. It's a shame no one realized your need for education when you were younger. For now, you need to rest and so do I. From what I've been told, Hodia wants to have some time with you tomorrow."

"What does she want of me?"

"I'll let her tell you, but I know it will be emotional. She's been doing some research on Henderson Ranch. That's all I know."

Chris thought about what Hodia could tell him the next morning. The boys at the ranch were the only people in his life from the time he was born until he aged out. Could they possibly be given the same opportunity he'd received? He hoped so. It saddened him to think Marco, as well as his friend, Peter, had aged out of the program. By now they were probably in Mexico doing manual labor on one of the ranches.

Chris' heart ached to think he might never again see any of the boys who had been constant companions in his life.

I can't continue to think this way. I can't change what is in the past, but my coming here could be the best thing for all of those who are still living in those conditions.

Chapter Six

Hodia reviewed the information President Addison sent to her on Monday morning. Henderson Ranch had been raided on Sunday and the conditions the authorities found had been appalling. The children there were undernourished and living in what could only be called filth.

The pictures she received made her sick to her stomach. How no one had investigated the place before this was beyond her comprehension.

"What is being done for these children?" she asked, when she contacted President Addison on her communicator.

"For now, they are in the custody of the federal government. I've been in contact with your contemporaries in Nevada and they are making arrangements for a facility like yours to take custody of them and give them a proper education. They will all be able to be children rather than slave labor."

"Have you been able to get any information on Chris' friend Marco?"

"Not yet, but we are working with the Mexican government. I was in conference with their president yesterday and he was as shocked at what we found as we were. He said he'd look into the ranches and see which ones are hiring young men who have aged out of Henderson. Hopefully, we can find Marco soon. I think it would be good for Chris' peace of mind."

~ * ~

Chris felt a bit apprehensive as he prepared for his meeting with Hodia. Last night, Cassion told him she wanted to talk about what she'd learned in her research on Henderson Ranch. He wasn't certain he wanted to know what she'd found out. In reality, he wished today would be another reading lesson or even one in mathematics. They would be much more relaxing than what he was about to hear.

Tentatively, he waved his hand to alert the door to open. Hodia was waiting for him and talking into her communicator. It was entirely possible she was having a private conversation and wasn't ready for him.

Instead, she motioned for him to come in and have a seat at the desk where he'd sat the day before. After finishing her conversation, she turned her attention to him. "I have news I think you might be interested in."

"Cassion told me you would be talking to me about Henderson Ranch. What do you want to know?"

"It's not what I want to know, it's what you need to know. On Sunday, a raid was made on the ranch. The conditions they found were deplorable and the food substandard. The Hendersons were taken into custody and the children were removed."

"What will they do with the kids? Will they be arrested?"

"Good heavens no. They are being medically evaluated and taken to one of our facilities in Nevada. Once all of the evaluations are made, they will be given the same opportunity as we have given you. Their educations will be addressed. President Addison sent some pictures. He would like you to look at them and identify as many of them as you can. If there are ones you know personally, you can give us an indication of what kind of education each of them should be given."

"What if you find families for them? Aren't they like me, unwanted?"

"No one is unwanted," Hodia replied, tears again forming in her eyes. "I want to find the people who have perpetuated this terrible myth. Hopefully, we can find families who are willing to work with us to right these wrongs."

Chris' mind spun with all the new information he was being given. Was it possible he had a family? If so, would they want him in their lives? If they didn't, he would have lost nothing. With the help of everyone at the complex he had the tools to build a new life for himself.

He waited while Hodia went to the printer to get hard copies of the pictures President Addison sent earlier. Listening to the printer doing its job, he became more and more apprehensive. How would he feel seeing pictures of the kids he left behind two years ago when he aged out of the program?

Seeing the pictures tore at his heart strings. He picked out familiar faces and identified them along with what their interests were. Seeing them, he realized how gaunt each of them looked. Had he been that thin when he lived at Henderson Ranch? He knew the answer was yes, but seeing the boys he'd grown up and worked with drove home the realization of what a proper diet could do.

After the good food he'd eaten at the complex, he knew what he had to eat at the camp was only a little better than at the ranch. The difference was he did get three meals a day. Instead of the manual labor of the ranch, he built muscle through exercise and training. The weight he gained while with Patrick and his group was more from empty calories and increased muscle mass.

"I don't know the younger ones, but there are two missing who should be there. Bobby and Jimmy were brothers who came there when they were four and five."

"Could someone have come and claimed them?"

"I doubt it. Even at such a young age they were rebellious. It's possible they didn't survive the punishment. There have been others who were there one day and gone the next. Marco and I were convinced they died. Sometimes the punishments could be very harsh."

"Can you describe the punishments?"

Chris didn't want to remember the hours he'd spent in the box, but he knew he needed to tell Hodia everything he could about the treatment the Hendersons gave to the children entrusted to their care.

"The little ones, the ones under the age of six were treated very well. Once we reached the age of six, we were expected to do the ranch work like everyone else. I started riding with the others when I was that age. If they decided we needed to be punished, there were severe paddling's and if that didn't work, we were put in the box. The first time I went into the box, I was six or seven. I was so hungry I stole a piece of bread from the kitchen. When Mrs. Henderson caught me, she gave me six paddles and turned me over to Mr. Henderson. He told me they didn't condone thievery and he put me in the box in the middle of the day. I was in there for what seemed like an eternity, but in reality, it was only about four or five hours. However long it was, I decided it was better to go hungry than to have to go back into the box. There were a few of the kids who didn't learn as quickly as I did. I remember one boy was in the box for three days and when they took him out, he was dead."

Hodia's expression was one of horror and disbelief. "Can you describe the box?"

Chris nodded. "It's a metal box, with a tight mesh screen on the door to let in some air. It's located behind one of the barns, away from where all the other activity takes place. They always choose the hottest day of the year to put someone in it. The confinement usually begins at noon when the sun is the hottest. For the first infraction, you stay in the box for four to five hours. Each time you are taken back there, the time is doubled. Most of us were smart enough to learn from the first experience but there were several who were so rebellious they went back again and again."

"What did they do with the bodies of the boys who died?"

"They were buried behind where the box was located. I'm positive if anyone looks, they will find many bodies, including those of Bobby and Jimmy."

Hodia didn't say anything, but activated her communicator. He listened as she contacted President Addison and advised him a thorough search of the property belonging to Henderson Ranch was necessary and they should be looking especially for any bodies buried there.

For the remainder of the morning, Chris helped Hodia to catalog and record all the information he could impart.

"I know you were looking forward to your class this morning, but you have all the time in the world for that. The information you gave me will help us build the case against Mr. and Mrs. Henderson. What you have to say will be very important at the trial."

The word trial filled Chris with fear. The last thing he wanted was to have to face Mr. and Mrs. Henderson again, but if the information he had would close down that horrible place, it would be worth any discomfort he might feel.

~ * ~

When Chris left to go down to the dining room for the noon meal, Hodia reviewed the recordings of what he told her earlier. The images they brought to her mind were some of the most horrific things she could ever imagine.

"How could these people perpetrate such atrocities against innocent children?" she said aloud, knowing she was the only one who could hear what she said.

Her communicator signaled a call was coming in. Turning her attention to the device on her wrist, she saw President Addison's face appear on the screen. She'd only contacted him less than an hour earlier. He couldn't possibly have information on the search of the ranch. There hadn't been enough time between when she informed him of what Chris told her and not for any investigation to find anything.

"I have some sad news to tell you," President Addison said. "After I spoke with you, the leader of the team searching the ranch reached out to me. Not only had they found the box, but they found the graves of at least fifteen children. It will take a while for the DNA to be processed, but everything Chris told you is true. The two boys he mentioned were among the ones they found. They were only recently buried and both showed signs of dehydration and starvation. The evidence is piling up with everything we find. In the house they found what could only be called a paddle with blood stains on it. It will be a miracle if these people aren't given the death penalty."

Hodia was, for a moment, at a loss for words. "I didn't want to believe what Chris told me this morning, but this proves it. These children need to be protected."

"I agree totally. I know Caroline is working on trying to find family for Chris, but I'm appointing a task force to begin researching the families of the other children we've rescued. I'll keep you informed on what we find."

The communication ended and Hodia got up from her chair. She knew she needed to eat, but she was afraid anything she put in her stomach wouldn't stay there long. She decided to talk to Dr. Gratan and get his thoughts on everything she'd learned this morning.

Chapter Seven

Several days passed and Chris became more and more comfortable with the classes he was taking. Along with reading and math, he'd been introduced to science. Everything he learned made him hungry to learn more.

Zora told him she'd never seen anyone progress so quickly. He was already reading many of the books she had deemed too advanced for him. Once he learned how to make the letters become words, he couldn't read fast enough.

Anxious for his next reading lesson, he hurried to the classroom. To his surprise, Caroline waited for him.

"I didn't expect to see you this morning," he said when he entered the room.

"I'm certain you didn't. From the files that were found at Henderson Ranch, we have learned quite a bit about your background before you went there to live. You were right about your parents. Your father died in the crash and your mother shortly after your birth. We have also found the doctor who was the first one to treat your mother. He's agreed to come here and help us fill in the gaps. He'll be here tomorrow. Do you want to meet him?"

"You know I do. Hopefully, he can tell me something about my mother. Have you found anything else out about me?"

"Not yet, but there are people who are researching your DNA. It won't be long before they will be able to access the proper databases and find someone who is related to you. I know waiting is hard, but we have to be patient. Rushing things could bring about false information."

Chris agreed. As much as he wanted family, he would be content meeting one of the last people who saw his mother alive and saved his life.

~ * ~

Dr. Parker was shocked when he was contacted by the Council of Intergalactic Affairs. As far as he could remember, he'd never treated anyone from the Alien community. When they told him they were researching Christopher Laughlin, he'd searched his memory until he brought forth the face of the young woman who came into his emergency room for treatment. Her injuries were so bad, he was certain she wouldn't live the night. The only thing he could do for her was to make certain her baby would be born and at least given a chance.

He remembered being asked what to name the child. At the time, the only thing he could do was to say he would gladly give the child his first name. As for the last name, he thought it only fitting to give him the name of the man who's ranch the craft crashed on.

He was more than willing to go to Denver and suggested they should contact Pete Laughlin, since he was the first one to find the victims of the accident.

This morning, he and Pete waited at the spaceport for the shuttle that would take them to Denver.

"How do you feel about meeting this child after twenty years?" Pete asked.

"I'm excited and apprehensive all at the same time. I know I did everything I could for that poor girl, but she lost her life in spite of it. Giving that boy your last name was my decision. I know I should have asked you first, but there was no time."

"I've never considered what you did as wrong. To be truthful, I was pleased to think I was able to be a part of his life, even though I never met him."

"The way it sounds, we'll be meeting him soon. I'm almost afraid to see what we find. Have you been watching the news about those atrocities they've found at the Henderson Ranch?"

Pete nodded. "The thought of how those children were treated is enough to turn my stomach."

~ * ~

"Are you ready for this?" Caroline asked as she accompanied Chris to one of the meeting rooms.

"I'm not sure. I'd much rather be in class. It was because of these people that I ended up at Henderson Ranch."

"Don't be so quick to pass judgment. I have a feeling neither of these men had a hand in where you ended up. The least you can do is listen to what they have to say."

Chris ran his fingers through the hair that was just starting to grow back in. He was thankful for how quickly his hair grew back. It wasn't as long as it had been when he left Henderson Ranch. To be truthful, it wasn't much over an inch long, but at least no one could call him a skinhead. If there was anything in his life that he regretted, it was joining up with Patrick and the others. Of course, if that hadn't happened, he would have never met these people who gave him a new lease on life. It was all too complicated for him to think about now. He had to focus his attention on the two men who were probably the last people to see his mother alive.

The room where Caroline took him was one he hadn't been in before. Instead of a long table with chairs for each of the people attending the meeting, there was an intimate setting area with comfortable chairs and couches.

Two men occupied the chairs. They both looked to be in their late fifties or early sixties. As soon as Chris and Caroline entered the room, they got to their feet. Chris assumed it was out of respect for Caroline, because in his entire life no one had ever stood out of respect for him.

"I'm Dr. Christopher Parker," the first man said as he extended his hand. "I was the one who gave you your first name. When you were born, I was told you had to have a name. Since I was the first doctor to treat your mother, I thought it was only fitting. She was in no condition to name you, so I took the responsibility on myself. To be truthful, you were so premature it was possible you wouldn't live through the night. I couldn't let you leave this world without a name."

"That explains my first name, but why didn't you give me your last name?"

The other man stepped forward. "I think this is where I come in. My name is Pete Laughlin. The hover craft with your parents crashed on my north ranch. I was the first one there. It was evident the man in the craft was dead and the unit itself was on fire. How the girl survived will always be a mystery. I guess God had a hand in it. It had to be his plan for you to be born into this world. I'm pleased to finally get to meet you. From what I can see you've grown into a fine young man."

"Thank you, sir. What I want to know is why you sent me to Henderson Ranch?"

Dr. Parker took over the conversation. "I had no dealings with that. About six months after you were born, the social worker came to me and told me because of the DNA showing you were a mixed racial child, you were unadoptable. She told me the only place that would take children like you was Henderson Ranch. At the time, none of us knew what a hellhole it was. If I could turn back time…"

"That's something that can't happen," Chris said. "Growing up like I did eventually led to me coming here. I've been given a great opportunity, even though I am a mixed racial child. The Hendersons called me a breed. I never knew what that meant but I knew it wasn't good. I didn't even know what a Native American was until I came here. I'm told I should be proud of my heritage, but I know nothing about it. I hope to learn more as I get further along with my education. I can only hope the kids they were able to rescue from that terrible place will have the same opportunity I've been given. What I do want to know is what can you tell me about my mother?"

"Perhaps we should all make ourselves comfortable," Caroline suggested. "I have a feeling this is going to be a long story."

Everyone took seats, the two gentlemen on the chairs they occupied when Chris and Caroline entered the room, leaving the couch for them.

"It was a beautiful spring afternoon. I was just heading up to the house for supper when I heard the explosion. By the time I got out to the pasture, the hover craft had crashed and the two occupants were lying on the ground. The young man, I assume he was your father, was already dead. The young girl was badly injured and I could tell she was pregnant. I only saw her for a little while, but I could tell she was young, too young to be in the state she was. From what I remember she was a tiny little thing."

Pete seemed to choke up when he finished his narrative. Chris could only imagine the retelling of the story was emotional for the older man.

"I guess this is where I take over," Dr. Parker said. "When your mother was brought in to the emergency room, I was told there had been no identification on her and she was admitted as Jane Doe. I knew she wasn't going to make it, but I hoped we could save her child. The doctor who did the surgery kept her alive long enough for you to be born. At the end of my shift, I asked about you. She said it would be a miracle if you lived. You were born so early; your organs hadn't had time to develop. It turned out you were a fighter, because after several months in the NICU you gained enough weight to go home. That was when the social worker decided it was best to send you to Henderson Ranch. Had I known what we do now about where you were going to be sent, I would have tried to stop it."

Chris wiped the tears from his eyes. "I think it was for the best. I like to think I was responsible for closing that place down. What I do want to know is why there wasn't any identification?"

"Whatever they had with them was burned up in the crash," Pete replied. "Your father's wallet must have been in the craft. What other belongings they had were mostly clothes that were thrown out of the craft. There weren't any papers and even if there were, they would have been burned to cinders. The sheriff thought we could identify them by the VIN number, but it was burned completely off. Without the VIN number the sheriff couldn't be positive, but he was certain it was a stolen vehicle. There was no way of knowing who either of them was."

"I've been unwanted all my life. Now I know my name isn't even mine. It's nothing new. I do promise you this, Mr. Laughlin, I plan to make you proud of the fact I carry your name, even though we aren't related by blood."

"Had I known what your future held, I would have insisted you come and live with my wife and me. The night you were born, I was told they gave you my last name, but you weren't expected to live. I never knew what actually happened to you until I got the call to come here and meet you today."

Chris was moved by Pete's admission. Had things been different, this man could have been his adoptive father.

"Do you and your wife have children?"

"My son, Junior, runs the ranch now. He and his wife built a house on the property about ten years ago and my wife and I still live in the main house. If you ever decide you'd like to come for a visit, we would be happy to welcome you with open arms. When I told Junior about this trip today, he said he wished you would have been brought out to the ranch. He would have loved to have had a little brother. His sister said the same thing. Damn, this is the hardest thing I've ever had to swallow in my entire life. I wish I could have been able to raise you the right way. I know this doesn't change anything. I hope you don't hold this against us."

"You had nothing to do with it, you either, Dr. Parker. You both tried to help my mother when there wasn't a chance of her surviving. I am grateful for the chance to thank you for everything you did to help her. Do you know what happened to her body, Dr. Parker?"

"As a Jane Doe, the procedure was to have her cremated. I'm sorry I can't give you the closure you need for having a grave. I'm afraid the same thing is possible for your father's remains, I'm certain they were also cremated."

Chris again thanked both of the men for coming. This was the link he was hoping would bring him some satisfaction and closure. Instead, it turned into another dead end. It was entirely possible no one would ever be able to tell him who his parents were.

Chapter Eight

Caroline was excited to start Chris' history classes. Her pregnancy was beginning to show and her husband, Aaron, worried about her doing too much. She kept telling him she hadn't ever felt as healthy in her life. Living at the complex she had the best medical care in the world and only the healthiest of foods.

"You're worried for nothing," she told Aaron. "I'm thrilled to finally be able to put my degree in history to work. Teaching isn't any more stressful than sitting around here wishing I was doing something productive. You'll see, this will work out well for me. It's only two days a week and only for two hours at a time."

"If you say so. All I'm saying is if you get too tired, I hope you will find another teacher to take your place."

Caroline shook her head. What Aaron didn't understand was that she was the most qualified person to teach Chris the history he never learned when he was a child.

~ * ~

"Are you ready for your history class this afternoon?" Cassion said while they were eating lunch in the dining room.

"I am, but I worry about Caroline. Melian said she's going to have a baby. Shouldn't she be resting or something. I mean, my mother died having me. I wouldn't want that to happen to Caroline."

"You do have a lot to learn. Did you even listen when Dr. Parker was here? Your mother died because of the injuries she sustained in the accident. Your birth had nothing to do with it. They did everything they could to keep her alive until you could be born."

"I understand," Chris replied, but in reality, he didn't understand anything other than he was someone no one wanted until he came here.

"Before you go to your class, I have some news for you. The people who have been researching your DNA have come up with two matches. The first is George Little Horse and his sister Susan Crow. The second is Chester Jennings and his sister Marie Jennings-Foster. It's entirely possible these four people could be the siblings of your parents. If they're agreeable, would you be interested in meeting them?"

A spark of excitement ignited in Chris' heart. "Do you think they want to meet me?" he asked.

"Anything is possible. George and his sister Susan live in northern Montana. I'm going to fly out there tomorrow to talk to them. Chester and Marie are living in Illinois, so Caroline's nephew, Tom Jamison, is going to be contacting them. We should know more by the end of the week."

Chris was afraid the news Cassion gave him was too good to be true. He decided not to dwell on it. He didn't want to get his hopes up only to have them dashed because he wasn't anyone special.

~ * ~

George Little Horse waited in his living room with his sister Susan for the man with the strange sounding name to arrive from Denver.

"Do you think it's possible these people could have actually found Juanita?" Susan asked.

"I told you, this man told me Juanita is dead. He thinks they've found her son. If you remember, the reason she left home with that boyfriend of hers was because she was pregnant and Pa couldn't abide her having had relations before marriage. You know how he was."

"I thought he kicked her out because of her white boyfriend."

"I don't think he was as concerned about him being white as he was about her going against the rules that he thought we should all live by."

A knock at the door interrupted their conversation.

George got up to answer the door. If he thought the name Cassion was strange, he now knew the reason why. The man was definitely an

Alien. He was at least seven feet tall and his violet eyes denoted his heritage.

"I'm Cassion," the man said, holding out a business card. "You must be George Little Horse."

"I am. Won't you come in? My sister and I have been waiting for you."

George knew Cassion's appearance was as much a shock to Susan as it had been for him.

"Your call wasn't quite clear. Do you have information about our sister, Juanita?" George asked.

"It's a long story," Cassion began. "Twenty years ago, there was a terrible hover craft crash on the Laughlin Ranch just outside of Sundance, Wyoming. The pilot, a young man, was killed in the crash. His passenger, a young woman, was thrown free. She was pregnant and, at the hospital, Dr. Parker kept her alive until her baby could be delivered. He was terribly premature and not expected to live. At the time he was born, Dr. Parker gave him the name of Christopher, for himself, and Laughlin for the ranch where the crash occurred. When the child survived, he was deemed to be unadoptable because of the fact he was of mixed race and he was sent to Henderson Ranch..."

Before he could finish, Susan screamed and began to cry hysterically. "H-how could anyone send a child to that hell hole? I've been reading about what went on there and it makes me sick to my stomach. Are you telling me my nephew endured those horrors?"

"Those and more. He was fair enough that he was able to pass as white and joined one of those skinhead groups in Idaho. It was when they began to protest outside of our compound that Chris was able to break away and begin to get the education as well as the nourishment he so badly needed. He is a highly intelligent young man. I have been teaching him mathematics and I've never had such a willing student. When he came to us, he could barely write his name, he couldn't read, and the only mathematics he knew was basic to say the very least."

"Can we meet him?" Susan asked, the question sounding more like a plea than anything else.

"I was hoping you would want to reconnect with Chris. He needs family more than anything else. Everyone at the complex has taken him under their wings, so to say. He's well liked, and it was because of what he told us that the raid on the Henderson Ranch was made and we were able to rescue several young boys. They have already been placed at our complex closest to the ranch and our researchers are trying to find the families who might be looking for them."

"Whenever you say we can go to Denver, my sister and I will be ready to leave," George said. "I run my own business and can leave anytime."

"For Chris' sake, I would like to have you come back to Denver with me. Would that work for you, Susan?"

George watched his sister's expression closely. "If you can give me an hour to make arrangements with my husband to take care of our kids, I'll be ready to go with you," Susan said.

"Do you have children to worry about, George?"

Cassion's question took George by surprise. "My wife is visiting her parents. They have a cabin in the mountains. I can let her and the kids know. I wasn't expecting them back until next week, but it's always best to let her know what's going on."

~ * ~

Tom Jamison wondered what he'd find when he visited Chester Jennings and his sister, Marie. The response he'd received when he called Chester on the phone was less than welcoming. It was entirely possible these people wanted nothing to do with a bi-racial relative.

He made the journey to Bloomington, Illinois, feeling less than optimistic about the outcome.

The house he went to was a modest home. Two hover craft were docked in the driveway. After landing his craft, he made his way up the sidewalk to the door. He didn't realize he was holding his breath until a man of about forty years of age greeted him. He had to look twice get over the shock of looking into the face of an older version of Chris.

"Are you Chester Jennings?" he asked, knowing full well his question was unnecessary. "I'm Tom Jamison. We spoke yesterday."

"I figured that's who you were."

A woman, who could have only been Chester's sister, Marie, appeared behind him. "Have you found Carter?" she asked.

Tom could hear the tears in her voice.

"Actually, no we haven't. I represent a young man who could possibly be his son."

"Son?"

The question came from inside the house and sounded like the voice of an older woman. If he expected to see a feeble old woman, he was mistaken. The woman was possibly in her early sixties. She was dressed in the latest fashion and her hair was meticulously styled.

"Mr. Jamison, this is my mother, Felica Jennings," Marie said, making the introductions.

They all went into the living room where Tom related the story of Chris' birth and the trials and tribulations he'd lived through his entire life.

"What can you tell me about your brother? Have you looked for him over the past twenty years?"

"Carter and his father had a falling out twenty-two years ago," Felicia explained. "He told us he was going out west and he didn't want us to look for him. He even went so far as to tell us we were dead as far as he was concerned."

"Mom and Dad didn't hear anything more from Carter, but I did," Marie said. "He told me he had a place in Wyoming and was doing very well. He even told me he'd met a girl by the name of Juanita and they were planning to get married. That was the last I ever heard from him. I figured he'd decided to lose himself somewhere in the mountains and he wanted nothing more to do with us."

For a moment the silence in the room was deafening. It was Chester who finally spoke.

"I can't believe that Carter is dead, but his son is alive. To hear he was brought up on that ranch that has been all over the news is enough to make me want to take matters into my own hands. Not only that but to know he was caught up in the skinhead shit. I wonder if I even want to meet him."

Tom began to smile. "I have no doubt you want to meet him. He is an extra special young man. According to my aunt, he is hungry for all the knowledge he was denied as a child. He has progressed from knowing only how to do the most basic of math and hardly being able to write his name, to reading at a high school level. He's embracing his studies in history and science as well."

"He sounds like Carter," Felica said, her voice hardly above a whisper. "He always had top grades. His father always said he was too smart for his own good. I think that's why they clashed so often. I know my late husband blamed himself for Carter's disappearance. To know Carter has been dead for over twenty years is a hard pill to swallow, but I want to meet my grandson."

"That's all well and good, Mom," Chester cautioned. "I'm worried about what this guy wants from us. We could be opening ourselves up to a scam."

Tom was appalled. "I assure you, when Chris started this journey, he had no hopes of ever finding family. All his life he's been told he was unwanted. If you're not sincere, I suggest you don't make the trip to Denver to see him. Before you come to any conclusion, you need to know, his mother was Native American. His being bi-racial was the reason he was sent to Henderson Ranch. The social worker at the hospital deemed him unadoptable, therefore she thought that was the only place for him."

Although Chester remained hard to read, both Marie and Felica wept openly.

"I don't know about you, Chet," Marie said, getting to her feet with her hands planted firmly on her hips, "but Mom and I are ready to go out to Denver to meet Chris. All I have to do is tie up a few loose ends here. I'm going to book a flight for the end of the week. If you want to come with us, you're welcome, but Mom and I will be leaving here as soon as possible."

Chapter Nine

Chris tried to concentrate on his studies, but the thought that both sides of his family had been located was so overwhelming he could think of nothing else.

"I can see your heart isn't into this today, Chris," Caroline said. "You've been hitting the books pretty hard since you got here. Why don't you take the rest of the day off? I heard from my nephew and he made contact with your father's brother, sister and mother. They were very receptive and are planning a trip here in the near future."

Chris could hardly believe his ears. The mysterious white side of his family had been found. Would Cassion have the same success with his mother's relatives? He hoped so.

Taking Caroline's suggestion, he sat aside the history papers she gave him. She was right, he had been studying too much. He needed some time alone.

Leaving the classroom, he crossed the compound to the church where he'd been attending Sunday services. Although he'd listened to the readings as well as the sermons, he didn't know if he believed in the One God as strongly as the people that he'd been living with did. If there was a god, why had he lived such a hellish life for the last twenty years?

The doors to the church were unlocked, as he knew they would be. Going inside, he sat down in one of the front pews. He knew he should form some sort of a prayer, but he had no idea where to begin.

You have always been under my watchful eye, a strange voice sounded in his head. *It was no coincidence that the skinheads brought you to this complex. It was time for you to get to know me and begin your new life.*

Shocked at what he heard within the confines of his mind, he raised his head and looked toward the altar where a beautiful cross hung.

"Did I actually hear your voice in my head, God?" he asked aloud.

Although he received no answer, he felt a peace encompass his entire being.

"I thought I heard someone in here," the pastor of the church said. "Is there something I can do for you?"

"I-I think I heard the voice of God. I've been coming here ever since I came to the complex, but I didn't know if I believed. Am I going crazy?"

"No, my son, you aren't going crazy. If God has chosen this time to make his presence known to you, you are blessed."

"Why me? I don't know anything about God or religion. As far as I know I was never baptized nor was I ever taken to church as a child."

"I have a feeling God has always been with you. Would you like to be baptized?"

"I think I would but I'd like to take some time to think it over. I need to know more about this before I commit to anything."

"I completely understand. Whenever you're ready, I'll be here waiting for you. In the meantime, let me give you some reading material about the One God. It should help you with your decision."

Chris took the pamphlet and returned to his apartment. He knew the pastor had been right. He needed to do some serious studying before taking the next step.

~ * ~

Melian was waiting for him when he returned to his apartment.

"Where have you been?" she asked. "Cassion returned with two people and has been looking all over for you. Caroline told him she gave you the afternoon off, but no one could find you."

"It's a long story," Chris replied. "I went over to the church to think."

Melian's eyes lit up at his statement. "I thought you didn't believe. I mean, Aunt Zora said she felt like you were only going through the motions."

"I was. I figured it was the only place where I could be alone to collect my thoughts. While I was there, I thought I heard a voice in my head. Don't think I'm crazy, but I think it was the One God. The pastor came in while I was there and he gave me some reading material. I have a lot to think over."

"Well, you better think fast, because Cassion has told everyone to be on the lookout for you. Whoever finds you is supposed to take you to the meeting room."

"Am I in trouble?"

His mind spun out of control remembering the punishments he'd endured when he lived on the ranch. What kind of punishment could he expect from Cassion for disappearing without telling anyone where he was going?

"Of course, you're not, silly. I think the people with Cassion are your family."

Family, the word was so unnatural to him and yet it was what he'd wanted for his entire life. Opening the door to his apartment, he went inside to leave off the papers from his history class as well as the pamphlet from the church.

~ * ~

Cassion was slightly annoyed to find that on this most important day of his life, no one could find Chris. After alerting everyone in the complex to see if anyone could find the boy, he ushered George and Susan into the meeting room where Chris met Dr. Parker and Pete Laughlin weeks earlier.

They had just seated themselves when Chris entered the room. From outside the door Cassion could see Melian. It was appropriate she had been the one to find him. They were close to the same age and it was entirely possible they had feelings for each other. He recalled the conversation he'd engaged in with Chris weeks ago about the sensations that were taking over his body whenever he was around Melian. He prayed nothing would come of it until they were old enough to make the decision to dedicate their lives to each other.

"I'm sorry you were concerned," Chris said when he entered the room. "I had a lot on my mind and I went over to the church to take some time to think."

As soon as the boy made his apology, Cassion saw him focus on the man and woman who were sitting in the overstuffed chairs that dominated the room.

~ * ~

Chris turned his gaze from Cassion to the man and woman sitting in the chairs. *Is this my family?* He silently questioned.

The man got to his feet. His Native American features reminded Chris of his own high cheekbones and dark hair. Although the man's skin was a darker shade of bronze, he felt an instant connection.

"I'm your uncle, George Little Horse, and this is your aunt, Susan Crow. Your mother was our older sister, Juanita."

"How could you not know what happened to her?" Chris asked, regretting the words as soon as they passed his lips.

"When our father found out she was pregnant and not married, he kicked her out of the house. The last we saw of her, she got into a hover craft with Carter Jennings." George paused, as if trying to collect his thoughts.

"It's okay, George," Susan said, "I can take it from here. Juanita was closer to George than to me because they were only a year apart in age. This has been hard for him. We pleaded with Pa to go after her, but he said no. He also said she'd be back because he'd kept all of her identification. He knew she couldn't do anything without proof of her identity. Only she didn't come home. I thought she'd let us know when she had the baby, but we never heard from her again. I'm so glad we were able to find you. I just wish we'd known when you were born. I know Pa would have softened and brought you back to raise you."

Chris was at a loss for words. He hadn't been unwanted as he'd always been told. These people were opening their hearts to him. He wished he hadn't left his history class today. If he hadn't gone to the church, he would have been there when George and Susan arrived.

"Are you sure you want me?"

The look on Susan's face was one of disbelief. "Why would we not want you?"

"Don't you know? I'm bi-racial. No one wants someone like that."

Susan began to cry. It was George who took over. "There's plenty of white blood in our family. We can trace things back for many generations and more of our ancestors have married into the white community than into that of the People. We are a proud race, and it was my grandparents who found each other and moved onto the reservation. At the time, they legally changed their last name to Little Horse, in honor of one of our past ancestors. Be you white or red, you are part of our family and from now on we will be proud to call you our nephew."

Susan got to her feet and held out her hand to Chris. "I never got to hold you when you were little. I want you to know you will never be too old for me to hold you and hopefully be the aunt who spoils you rotten, if you allow me to."

He could feel her tears soaking into his shirt. Suddenly, he wasn't a twenty-year-old man, he was a little boy who needed someone to love him. Now this stranger was offering not only her unconditional love, but wanting him to be part of her family. He had no idea what being Native American meant. He prayed George and Susan would be able to teach him everything he needed to know.

"It's been a long day for all of us," Cassion said. "Why don't we go to the dining room for dinner? I contacted the kitchen staff when we were looking for you, Chris. They're preparing a special dinner for you and your family. I also thought you would like your privacy, so I arranged for you to eat in one of the private dining rooms."

"Can Melian join us?" Chris asked, suddenly thinking he wanted someone familiar with him as he got to know his new found family.

"Would you like to join us, young lady?" George asked. "I can see by the look in my nephew's eyes, you are someone who is important to him. I think having you with us will be more relaxing for him."

"Do you think it's alright, Cassion?" Melian asked.

Chris wanted to shout that he needed Melian with him, but it was Cassion who had always been the voice of reason. If he didn't think it was the proper thing to do, Chris knew he would abide by his decision.

"If your family is comfortable with Melian joining you, I don't see any reason why she shouldn't eat dinner with you and your family. I trust you will be on your best behavior, young lady."

Chris almost laughed out loud at Cassion's admonishment of Melian. She wasn't a willful child who needed to be reminded to be good. She was a young woman who he knew would never do anything to embarrass anyone.

"I promise. Thank you for inviting me, Mr. Little Horse."

"None of that. I'm Uncle George or just plain George if you're not comfortable calling me Uncle. I can tell you're important to my nephew. I think it's important for us to get to know you at the same time we get to know him."

Chris felt even more comfortable with his new family. It meant a lot that his Uncle George listened to his request to have Melian join them for the evening meal. He needed someone familiar to him by his side as he acquainted himself with these people who wanted to be his family.

Together they went into the private dining room. It was another of the rooms Chris had never been in before. He was in awe of the round table that had been set with five places. He wondered how the staff had been able to adjust the seating arrangement so quickly when the decision for Melian to join them had so recently been made. He was also impressed at the intimacy of what he considered a small table. Never before had he eaten at a table that wasn't large enough to accommodate up to ten people at the same time.

He watched as George held the chair for Susan and followed his example by holding Melian's chair. From the expression on Cassion's face, Chris knew he did the proper thing. All of this was so new to him. Sitting at a small table with individual chairs was far different form the long tables with benches for everyone to crowd in. It wasn't as cramped at the dining room at the complex, but none the less, it was far different from this set up.

Cassion quickly took the seat between Melian and George with Susan sitting on the other side of Melian, leaving only the chair between George and Susan for him.

"Can we say grace before we eat?" Susan asked.

Her request to say grace brought back memories of the time he'd sat at the church and listened to the voice of the One God in his head. *Is this normal?* he silently asked. Rather than an answer to his question, he felt the same warmth he'd experienced earlier in the day.

"Dear God, thank you for this day when you brought our nephew Chris back into our lives. Since our sister rests in your loving care, we thank you for keeping her son alive to complete our family. Also, thank you for these new friends who have taken such good care of him since he arrived here. They are doing your work. We give thanks for this meal that has been prepared for us. In Jesus' name, Amen."

Chris raised his head. He found he was in awe of the words his aunt spoke. He never expected her to pray for anything other than the food they were about to eat.

"Cassion told us about your childhood," George said, once their food was served. "I blame our father for that. He had a terrible temper. When Juanita was leaving, I begged him to go after her and apologize. He kept saying he'd kept her identification on purpose so that she would come back, but she never did. The last I saw of her she was getting into Carter's hover craft."

"What was my father like?"

"He was like the brother I never had. I looked forward to him becoming part of our family. It was hard growing up with two sisters and not a brother. Although you have your mother's eyes, I see a lot of Carter in you. He was smart and I'm told you are too. Juanita, on the other hand, was impulsive. She was more like me. She wanted things when she wanted them and wasn't willing to wait for them. I have a feeling that was the way she felt about Carter. She wanted him in her life and I think she decided the only thing she could do was to get pregnant. She should have known how our father's temper would boil over."

Hearing his uncle speak of his father in a positive way came as much of a surprise as hearing George describe his mother as impulsive. At the ranch, his impulsive behavior got him little more than punishments both by Mr. and Mrs. Henderson.

"Where are you originally from, Melian?" Susan asked, moving the conversation in a different direction.

"I was born at the complex under the ice cap at Antarctica. My mother thought it would be a good idea if I accompanied my Aunt Zora here when she came with Dr. Gratan. Aunt Zora is my mother's younger sister. We're actually closer in age than she is to my mother. I've enjoyed being here and helping with Chris' lesson plans. I want to be a teacher, be it on the surface or under the ice cap."

Chris was shocked when he heard Melian say she was helping with his lesson plans. He knew her desire to be a teacher but had no idea of the part she was playing with his educational needs.

"Have you given any thought to what you want to do with your life, Chris?" George asked.

"To be honest, I never had any plans for the future. All I knew when I came here was ranching and carpentry. I didn't like either of those options. When I fell in with Patrick's group, I thought maybe that would be what I was doing, but after coming here, I realized it was counterproductive. I'm only now learning the things I should have known for years. Even with so little education under my belt, I'm thinking I would like to work with kids in some capacity. I don't think I could be a teacher, like Melina, but maybe there would be something else I could do."

"There would be a place for you on the reservation," Susan said. "I work at a school and I think you would have a lot to share with the kids. I won't deceive you, some of those kids are very troubled. It's been that way on the reservation for longer than any of us like to think about, but we're working hard to overcome it."

Chris let the ideas his aunt planted in his head resonate. Her suggestion sounded good to him, but he knew he needed a lot more education before anything like that could happen. He also knew there was another side of his family who had been contacted. It was entirely possible they would have other ideas for what his future should look like.

"It is good to see your desire to reconnect with Chris," Cassion said. "I tend to agree with him, he has to decide what he wants to do on his own. Once his education here is complete, I'm certain he will make the best choice as to what to do with his life. You should also know, I learned that his father's family has been contacted and they are planning to visit the complex to get to know him."

"I'm shocked," George admitted. "Carter always told me he had no family. Do you know when they're going to be here. I'd like to be able to meet them and hear their side of the story."

"You're welcome to stay here for as long as you like. From what I've been told, those from the other side of his family will be here by the end of the week. If that will work into your schedule, I'm sure they will enjoy meeting you as well."

Chris had his doubts about what Cassion was saying. If his father denied having a family, how would they feel about sharing their time at the complex with George and Susan?

Chapter Ten

On Friday morning, Chris had finished his class when he was summoned to the meeting room. He knew it was because his father's family had arrived. George and Susan told him they were going to be busy with a tour of the complex given by Hodia and Caroline.

He wished Melian was going to be with him, but she was also going with George and Susan. Today he would be meeting his father's family alone. He hoped he was up to the challenge.

When Cassion said the Jennings family were coming to meet him, he asked to meet them alone. It had been different when he met his mother's family. He hadn't known what to expect or what questions to ask.

Spending the past few days with George and Susan had bolstered his confidence. He was a grown man and didn't need someone to hold his hand. Even so, his stomach was in knots and his nerves were kicking into high gear.

He stood in front of the closed door, knowing the minute he opened it he would be confronted by his father's family. Why had he told George his family was dead? Was he a rebellious young man who had been an embarrassment to his family? Were the authorities right when they accused him of stealing the hover craft that crashed and took his life?

Tentatively, he waved his hand to gain entrance to the meeting room. As soon as the door slid open, he gasped. The man sitting in one of the chairs looked like an older version of himself, except his hair was light brown with a smattering of grey at the temples.

Forcing himself to look away, he saw an older woman who was, more than likely, his grandmother, sitting next to a younger version of herself.

"I'm Chester Jennings," the man said, getting to his feet and extending his hand. "Your father, Carter Jennings, was my brother. This is my sister, Marie Jennings-Foster and my mother, Felica Jennings."

"I'm pleased to meet you. Is there a reason your father isn't with you?"

He could see tears forming in his grandmother's eyes. "My husband, your grandfather, passed away about three years ago. I had no idea your father was also dead. I'm hoping the two of them are together and they have patched up their differences."

"What kind of differences?" Chris asked, knowing full well that his question was probably hurtful for his grandmother.

"Carter and Dad had a falling out when my brother said he didn't want to work in the family business," Marie said. "He said he was too smart to work in a factory and Dad told him to get out. Chester heard from him, but the folks and I didn't. The last any of us knew, he had a place in Wyoming. After that we heard nothing."

Chris sat down in the chair next to his uncle. "Did they tell you my father was killed in a hover craft accident?"

"They did."

"I was told the authorities thought it was stolen."

"Stolen?" Felica echoed. "Carter wouldn't steal anything. He worked hard to buy his hover craft. It was old, but he was able to pay cash for it. That was one of the things he and his father fought over. My husband thought he should have waited until he could afford a new one, but Carter wanted his independence. I think buying the one he did was just another one of his rebellious actions that led to him leaving our home."

Chris recalled George telling him about the older model hover craft Carter had when he and Juanita left her father's home on that fateful day.

"I didn't want to think about my father being a thief," Chis admitted. "I'm relieved to have you confirm it for me."

"Where do you see your life going from here?" Marie asked.

Chris smiled. "It seems my mother's sister asked me the same thing earlier in this week. I have a long way to go before I can make any decisions. I missed out on an education when I was a child and now I'm trying to make up for lost time. I think I want to work with children but that all could change. One of my teachers, Caroline, says I could change my mind several times before I know exactly what I want to do."

"Good for you," Chester said, reaching over to pat Chris on the back. "Your father was too smart for his own good, at least that's what Pa said. It was one of the reasons they clashed so easily. Take your time. You don't have to make up your mind right away."

"Would you consider coming to Illinois to visit us?" Felicia asked.

"I'd have to think about it. I'm just getting used to having family. I met my mother's family earlier this week. They want me to come to Montana to see them as well. I will probably come to see you as well as them, but it won't be right away. For now, I'm busy with my studies and a few other things."

He was careful not to mention his growing feelings for Melian or his new found interest in God and the church. He also didn't want to bring up the trial that would be held for the Hendersons. Until he was certain they were where they would never harm another child, he couldn't make any concrete plans for the future.

He'd been told they could eat lunch in the same private dining room where he'd met with his mother's family earlier in the week. He wished Cassion would be with him, but he'd been the one who said he could handle this meeting privately. The warm feelings he felt for Uncle George and Aunt Susan certainly weren't the same for Uncle Chester. The man seemed to be cold, even stiff, in his demeanor. If Felica's husband was anything like this man, it was no wonder his father left and told everyone they were dead.

Aunt Marie and his grandmother were entirely different. He actually liked them and wanted to get to know them better.

Once they were in the dining room, his grandmother insisted he sit between her and Marie. It was a relief not to have to sit next to Chester. It was bad enough to have the man glaring at him from across the table.

"Can we say grace?" Chris asked when no one else volunteered to do so.

Felicia and Marie clasped hands with him. He noticed Chester was reluctant to do so, but finally took both his sister and mother's hands.

"Heavenly Father," Chris began, "thank you for bringing both sides of my family to meet me. Bless this food and the hands that prepared it. In Jesus' name, Amen."

He waited for the warm feeling of peace, but he was in too much turmoil to experience it.

Dear God, he silently prayed, *help me to embrace this family in the same way as I have my mother's family. This is what I've wanted for my entire life. Help me, Lord. Amen.*

~ * ~

Melian wondered how Chris' meeting with his father's family was going. When he said he wanted to meet them alone, she worried, but decided to abide by his wishes. Instead of going with him she had joined George and Susan on their tour of the complex.

"I'm impressed with this facility," Susan said when they returned to the dining room for the noon meal. "Everyone I've met today has been very welcoming and it's evident Chris is well respected here as well."

"He is," Melian agreed. "It's not hard to respect him. Coming from the background that he did, he's adapted well to our way of life. I have to admit when I first met him, I had my doubts. He was wearing those terrible fatigues and I was certain he hadn't showered in several days. His head was also shaved and he had a beard. I'm so glad he shaved and let his hair grow back. Sometimes I wish I could get inside his mind and know what he's thinking about."

"What do you mean?" George asked.

"I think he has such bad memories of that horrible place where he grew up that they haunt him. He had a good friend there, but so far no one has been able to locate him. I think he is worried about what might have happened to him. I know when he learned about the bodies they found buried on that farm, it weighed heavily on his mind."

"Bodies?" Susan echoed. "I didn't hear anything about that."

Melian realized she might have spoken out of turn, but it was too late. The words had passed her lips and couldn't be taken back. She related the story Chris told her about the box and how some of the children didn't survive it.

"How could anyone be so cruel?" George asked. "I knew about the deplorable conditions they found when they raided the place, as well as the crap they were making those kids eat, but I didn't think it went as far as murder. That's what it is after all. It's out and out murder. If you ask me those monsters deserve the death penalty."

"The way I see it, it's a good thing no one asked you, George," Susan said. "You know as well as I do that the death penalty was abolished over fifty years ago. We'll have to let the courts decide the fate the two of them will suffer."

Melian agreed. She was glad they were now seated in the dining hall and their meal was served. She certainly wasn't comfortable talking about the conditions on Henderson Ranch.

~ * ~

Chris was relieved when the tense lunch was over. He needed time to put everything in perspective. Making the excuse he had a class he needed to attend, he left them to explore the complex or perhaps go to the rooms that had been set aside for them.

Caroline waited for him in the classroom. He wondered if she thought he would actually show up, considering his father's family arrived earlier in the day.

"Are you sure you should be here?" Caroline asked. "I mean, didn't you meet with your father's side of the family this morning?"

"I did, but I'm very confused. I needed to come and learn more history."

"I don't think you need a history lesson as much as you need to talk. What's bothering you?"

Chris hung his head. He knew he should be as thrilled to meet the Jennings side of his family as he had been meeting George and Susan. It just wasn't the same.

"I don't have any ill feelings for my Aunt Marie or my grandmother. It's Uncle Chester who bothers me. He seems very cold. It's like he wishes I'd never been found."

Caroline shook her head, a look of dismay on her face. "It was my nephew, Tom, Dr. Jamison's father, who made contact with them. When I talked to him after he met with them, he said he felt Chester was rather cold. He got the impression that, if it hadn't been for Marie and Felicia insisting he come out here, he would have been content to stay in Illinois. Maybe you should skip class today and meet with your aunt and grandmother privately. I can arrange for Cassion or maybe Dr. Gratan to keep Chester busy. Why don't you go back to your apartment and let me see what I can do?"

Chris was relieved to think he wasn't the only one who thought Chester was a cold and angry man. "I'd appreciate that."

He left the classroom and made his way to the elevators. Not seeing any of his Jennings family, he was relieved when the doors silently closed and he was alone in the moving cubical.

Once he arrived at his floor, he made his way to his apartment. For the first time all day, he was alone with his thoughts. Sitting down on the couch, he closed his eyes in the hopes of putting all of his feelings into perspective.

Suddenly, the peace he'd wanted to feel after saying grace encompassed him. He didn't know he'd fallen asleep until dreams filled his mind.

"I'm your father," the man in his dream said, *"and this is your mother. I wanted to be a better father to you than my father was to me. He ran a manufacturing plant and wanted me to work there with him. I wanted more and I found it when I met your mother.*

"I never expected her father to kick her out of the house when we told him she was going to have my baby. We were almost to my apartment in Sundance when she realized she didn't have her identification. She wanted to go back to get it."

"Let me take the story from here, Carter," the woman in the

dream continued. *"I was so upset when I realized my father hadn't given me my identification, I tried to turn the craft around. That was when we lost control and crashed.*

"Even though I was unconscious, I knew what was going on. God allowed me to see you being born. Once I heard you cry, God took me to be with Carter.

"My family wants to get to know you, please let George and Susan into your life."

His father again appeared to take over the narrative. *"Chester is just like my dad. He's a hard man to get to know. Let Mom and Marie get to know you. Chester will come around, but it's possible he's intimidated by your incredible mind. That was what went wrong between my father and me. Maybe we could have worked things out, but we never got the chance."*

The Chris in his dream wanted to ask more questions, but someone ringing the bell requesting entrance to his apartment abruptly woke him.

Shaking his head, he got up and waved his hand to open the door. As soon as it slid open, he saw Caroline standing there with his Aunt Marie and his grandmother.

"May we come in?" his grandmother asked.

He nodded. His head was still blurry from the dream he'd experienced when he had no intention of falling asleep.

"I was able to get someone to take Chester on a tour of the facility, so you could talk with Marie and Felica alone," Caroline said. "I don't think you need me here and I promised Aaron I would come home and take a nap." She winked broadly as she turned to leave the apartment.

"I can't believe Chester was such an ass when we met with you earlier," Marie said. "I think he was always jealous of your father. Carter had a brilliant mind and always got top grades. Chester couldn't measure up with his grades so he excelled in sports."

"My husband wanted Carter to be a star on the football or basketball team, but that wasn't what interested him," Felica said, with tears in her eyes. "It put a wedge between Carter and Chester as well as my husband. Chester was the son your grandfather wanted. He enjoyed his sports and he loved working with his hands. He could never understand why your father wasn't interested in the same things."

Chris took a moment to digest what he'd just been told. "I have a feeling he wishes I was never found. Until I came here, I knew nothing about grades and I certainly had no interest in sports. I was brought up being taught the only thing that mattered was hard work. It's been the people here who have instilled in me the love of learning. I'm sorry if I'm not the nephew my uncle wants."

"He'll come around," Marie said. "For now, know that you're the nephew and grandson Mother and I want. Will you allow us to better acquaint with you as well as the other people here? You have no idea how much I've missed Carter all these years. I have kids and so does Chester, they're your cousins. Hopefully, when you know what your life will hold, you will allow us all to get to know you."

Marie's words touched Chris' heart. "All my life, I was told no one wanted me. I have mixed feelings about Uncle Chester but I'll keep an open mind where he's concerned. My mother's brother and sister are here also. Would you like to meet them?"

His grandmother was the one to answer. "Chester told me he'd heard from Carter and that he'd met a young woman he wanted to be his wife. I envisioned their wedding and wept openly when I thought I would never meet her or any children they might have. Now I know a wedding wasn't in either of their futures, but I have another handsome grandson who needs my love. I would be honored to meet the other side of your family, since they were, probably, the last people to see my son alive."

"I agree with my mother," Marie said. "We've had a lot to digest in the past few days. Meeting your aunt and uncle will help me put things into perspective. Now, I think it would be best if I took Mother to her room so she can get some rest. We will meet you tonight for dinner."

Chris bid them both good-bye and wondered if he had the right to suggest a meeting between the two sides of the family he never knew existed. He had no doubts that his aunt Marie and grandmother would get along with Uncle George and Aunt Susan, but he worried about Uncle Chester. He was so cold when they met, he worried about the man allowing his prejudices and surly attitude to taint the meeting.

Unable to think about it any longer, he went into his bedroom to choose what he would wear for this evening's meal, before taking a shower. Since coming to the complex, he learned how much he enjoyed being clean. He found his mind became clearer and he did his best thinking when he allowed the hot water to pound his body and remove the worries of the day from his mind.

~ * ~

The private dining hall looked more like a highly decorated reception area than the room where Chris met both sides of his family hours and days earlier. He was glad he'd chosen one of the suits Cassion suggested he add to his wardrobe. Although he knew he'd be much more comfortable in the clothes he wore every day, the suit seemed to fit the occasion.

Caroline and Aaron met him at the door. Each of them wore formal attire. "I am so glad you suggested both sides of your family meeting. Marie told me of your decision and I decided to make it a special celebration."

"Thank you, but…"

"There are no buts, my boy," Aaron said, after shaking his hand. "This is a marvelous idea. Everyone at the complex is thrilled with, not only the progress you have made since your arrival, but also the fact Hodia and her team were able to find the members of both sides of your family. Cassion and Hodia, along with Zora and Melian are also special guests for tonight's banquet. They, along with Caroline and myself, have become the third side of your family. Tonight is about the blending of all of the people who have been, and will become, very important in your life."

Chris thought about what Aaron said. With all of the people who were gathered here, he knew one other important person in his life was missing. Although his memories of his days at Henderson Ranch were tainted with the atrocities that went on there, his one true friend had been

Marco. Had he lived long enough to age out of the ranch? Was he working on a ranch in Mexico or had his rebellious nature sent him to the box? If it had, was his one of the bodies found when the area surrounding the box was excavated?

With no answer's forthcoming, Chris forced himself to smile and scan the room to see how the members of his family were communicating with each other.

Susan, Felica and Marie were standing together talking and laughing. It was evident the three of them were quickly making a bond that could be called friendship. In direct contrast were George and Chester. It looked as though they were engaged in a serious discussion. On the fringes were the aliens, along with Caroline and Aaron. It was as if they were monitoring the meeting, always on the alert for open hostilities to break out at any moment.

"I didn't think you'd ever get here," Melian said, as she came to his side. "You are, after all, the guest of honor tonight."

"I'd much rather be in the main dining room with the people I've made friends with," Chris groused, running his fingers under his shirt collar, as though his tie was too tight.

"Stop it," she admonished. "You look so handsome tonight. I spent today with your uncle and aunt and I found them to be great people. I did meet your other aunt and your grandmother. They are so excited to be here and have had the opportunity to get to know you."

"You didn't mention Uncle Chester. What do you think of him?"

"He's very hard to read. I think he needs to take his time in getting to know people before he's comfortable. They've been arguing about which one of your parents you favor."

"Chris, come join us," George called, before he could comment on Melian's observations.

Reluctantly, he joined his two uncles who were in such direct contrast to each other.

"George says you favor your mother, while I think you're the exact replica of my brother." Chester said.

"We've been discussing the same thing," Felica said, as the

women joined the conversation. "We each want to see our lost loved one in you. I do say I can see my son in your coloring but after seeing the pictures of your mother, I see her in your eyes as well as your smile. I think you are a perfect combination of both sides of your family."

His grandmother's mention of pictures came as a surprise. In both of his meetings with his family, he hadn't seen or even heard of any pictures. He longed to see the faces of the people who gave him life. Would he be able to pick out familiar features or would he only see strangers? The mention of his smile reminded him of how he could never remember smiling before he came to the complex. Living at Henderson Ranch, as well as with Patrick and his group, he couldn't remember having anything to smile about.

Felica handed him a picture of his father. He could see some similarities. It was Susan who handed him a picture of his mother. His grandmother was right, the eyes that stared back at him were the same ones he saw in the mirror every morning when he shaved. He couldn't attest to the smile, because he never smiled when he was shaving and that was the only thing he did in front of the mirror.

He closed his eyes for a moment and recalled the two people he'd seen in his dream. Miraculously, they were the same two people from the pictures he held in his hand. Having died within hours of each other they were, undoubtedly, together for all eternity.

"It's overwhelming, isn't it?" Marie asked.

Unable to get any words past the lump in his throat, he merely nodded his head.

"I think it's best if you sit down and get something to eat. Susan will go over and get you a plate of appetizers."

"Why did they have to die? Why weren't they able to be happy and raise me in a good home?" Tears he'd never been allowed to shed as child rolled down his cheeks, making his words more of a sob than a question.

"I can't tell you what happened, but I have a good idea," Susan said, as she set the plate with food he didn't want to eat. "Pa told us he kept her identification so he knew she would be back. I have had a dream, ever since we were told you'd been found. In it, Juanita came to me and said the accident was her fault. She wanted to come back for her identification and grabbed the controls making the hover craft crash. It makes sense to me. She would have been horrified when she realized she didn't have her identification. When she didn't come back, I had a feeling she would never return. I prayed every night that she was happy with Carter. I guess she is, but not on the earthly plain."

Tears that seemed to come so easily lately, flowed down his cheeks. His earlier sobs were acting as a release. For the first time he was mourning his parents.

"I don't think it's productive to dwell on the past," Felica said. "There is nothing we can do to change anything that happened back then. For now, we need to show Chris he has two families who love him. Everything is completely new to him and he must decide what is best for him as he goes forward with his life. If I had my way, I'd bring him back to Bloomington with me and never let him out of my sight again. Of course, I know that's not what's best for him. Everyone here at the complex has been good to him and I, in no way, could take him away from such a positive influence."

"Well said, Mom," Chester replied. "I know I come off as a cold fish and a hard ass, but as much as I'd like to get to know you, Chris, I understand everything these people have done for you has been for the best."

Chris wiped away the last of his tears. Once he had his emotions under control, he said, "It has been for the best. I watched two of the young men I trained killed when we protested here at the complex. I also knew that the Hendersons were responsible for killing many of the boys who were at the ranch. They were there one day and gone the next. We all knew better than to ask what happened to them. Cassion and everyone else here has given me more than an education. They've given me a future. I do want to get to know both sides of my family, but it will take time for any kind of a bond to form. For now, let's enjoy this banquet my friends here at the complex have arranged."

Once everyone found their seats, it wasn't surprising to have both sides of his family sitting next to each other. George, Marie, Chester and Susan were seated on one side of the table, with Chris, Felica, and Melian on the opposite side. At another table were Cassion, Hodia, Aaron, Caroline and Zora. Chis was certain his friends from the complex were congratulating themselves for how well the reunion with his family went.

Chapter Eleven

After an emotional reunion with both sides of his family, Chris was relieved to have his life return to normal.

With each class, he felt himself growing in more ways than he expected. Every book he read shed light on what he'd missed by being denied an education when he was younger. He was especially interested in the Native American history classes he'd been taking with Caroline.

As each month passed, he marveled at the changes taking place in Caroline's body. Living at the ranch, he'd never seen a pregnant woman, or even understood relations between a man and a woman. He worried about the amount of time she spent teaching him. From his conversations with Aaron, he agreed she should be resting rather than planning lessons.

"I was able to find some very old history books," Caroline said when he entered the classroom for the afternoon session. "I have no idea how they were found, but I think you will enjoy reading them. The top one is the history of the battle at the Little Big Horn and the second is a history of the Cheyenne people, written by a chief who lived at the beginning of the twentieth century. I read through it, last night, and found it to be one of the best representations of the Cheyenne I've been privileged to study. If you want to take them back to your apartment, feel free to. I saw Dr. Gratan this morning and he wants me to come back for more tests this afternoon."

"Is the baby okay?" Chris asked, anxiety building within him.

"The baby is fine. Because of my age he wants to do some testing to make certain everything is progressing as it should. You're beginning to sound like Aaron. I swear the male of the species never changes. I'm pregnant, not an invalid. It was the same with my first husband when I was expecting our daughter."

Chris was bewildered. Caroline never mentioned having a

daughter before. Of course, it had been over a hundred years earlier. "You had a daughter? Did you leave her when you went into suspended animation?"

"No, she died many years before I made that decision. It happened shortly after her birth and no matter how hard we tried I was not able to have another baby. It's a miracle Aaron and I were able to conceive this child. I plan to do everything in my power to make certain it is healthy at the time of its birth. It seems the suspended animation made many changes in my body, or maybe it was God's will that I bring forth new life in the middle years of my life."

Chris contemplated Caroline's mention of God. With all the excitement of reuniting with his family, he'd had little time to study the pamphlet the pastor gave him. Considering he would have a free afternoon, he might be able to read not only the suggested material from Caroline, but also the pamphlet that had been lying on his desk for several days.

~ * ~

Back in his apartment, the first book he opened was the one written by the Cheyenne chief. The history of the once proud people filled him with excitement to know these were his ancient ancestors. It was the coming of the white man that began the decline of their lifestyle.

"Why didn't you intervene when all of this was happening, God?" Chris implored.

As soon as the words left his mouth, he became too exhausted to stay awake any longer. Lying down on the sofa, he decided he would close his eyes for just a short rest.

You are learning the history of this country, my son. What happened with the Native Americans is what has been happening to people who were different since the beginning of time.

Perhaps it is my fault for giving people free will. Over many millennia, different groups have decided they were superior to others. The atrocities that were done against the Native Americans were as wrong as was the extermination that was carried out in Germany during the second world war.

Talk to the pastor and add the reading of the Bible to your classes. He will be able to answer any questions you will have about what you have read. You will learn that wars have been raging upon the earth ever since the beginning of time.

Trust in me and the wrongs will become right. You, like Caroline, will be very important in the future. You may not see it now, but soon it will be evident.

The dream faded and Chris slipped into a deep sleep. It wasn't until his communicator signaled a message coming through that he woke.

He glanced down at his communicator and saw the worried expression on Cassion's face. "Are you all right?" the older man asked, once Chris opened the connection.

"Yes, yes of course. I was doing the homework Caroline assigned for me. I became so tired, I laid down and took a nap. I guess I overslept."

"You most certainly did. You missed dinner, entirely. Now that I know there is nothing wrong, I will bring up a plate for you."

Chris got up from the sofa and looked out the window. It was no wonder Cassion was concerned. It was dark outside and his communicator told him it was after eight. He was surprised to think hunger hadn't awakened him. He usually went down to the dining room no later than six in the evening.

Before he could even go into the bathroom to splash water on his face to wash the sleep from his eyes, Cassion was at the door.

He waved his hand and the door opened. The aroma of the food Cassion carried on the tray made his stomach growl in anticipation of what he would soon be eating.

"You must have been exhausted to sleep through dinner," Cassion greeted him.

"I didn't think I was that tired, but when I finished reading the book Caroline gave me about the Cheyenne, I voiced my opinion and asked God how something like that could happen. Suddenly, I was so tired

I couldn't stay awake. As soon as I fell asleep, I had a dream that God was speaking to me."

Cassion's expression turned to one of apprehension. "How did you know it was God and not your overactive imagination?"

"I knew because I heard him speaking to me before."

Chris seated himself on the sofa and set the plate of food on the table beside him.

"When did he speak to you?"

He swallowed down the mouthful of food he'd taken before answering. "The day when no one could find me, I went to the church to have some quiet time to think. It was then that he first spoke to me. It was the same voice I heard in my dream today. He wants me to go to the church and ask the pastor for a copy of the bible. He wants me to read it and pose any questions I might have to the pastor."

Cassion smiled. "You are indeed blessed. It's been a long time since I've heard of anyone hearing the voice of the One God. My father told me of how my grandfather started making plans for this complex before we left the dark side of the moon."

"I thought all of the aliens came from under the ice pack of Antarctica."

"That's where Hodia's family came from. The One God has outposts on many different planets and satellites throughout the galaxy. My people as well as Hodia's have been monitoring everything done on Earth for many generations. It wasn't until the One God told us the time was right to make our presence known that we were able to come here and start building various complexes around the globe."

"Why do you think he has chosen to speak to me? I'm not one of the aliens or anyone else that is important."

Cassion sat, quietly contemplating his answer while Chris continued eating his dinner. "You are a very intelligent young man. That said, you have also lived an interesting life. You survived the horrors of your childhood and the regimentation of being with Patrick's group is almost a miracle. We have been blessed to be entrusted with your education. I think the reason the One God is speaking to you is that he has great plans for your future. Take your time and learn everything you can. Once you are comfortable with yourself, you will be ready to decide what the future holds for you."

~ * ~

If Chris thought he wouldn't be able to sleep after his afternoon nap, he was mistaken. When Cassion left, he'd picked up the remainder of his reading material to continue his studies, but found he couldn't concentrate.

Instead of trying to force himself to study, he went into the bedroom and prepared for bed. It seemed as though he no more than laid his head against the pillow than he was asleep.

No dreams, at least none that he remembered, invaded his subconscious giving him the rest his body craved. The next morning, he awoke, completely rested.

After taking care of his morning needs, he dressed and went down to the dining hall to enjoy breakfast before his classes started for the day.

Melian met him as soon as he got off the elevator. "I missed you last night," she greeted him.

"I'm afraid I fell asleep. Cassion brought dinner up to my apartment and we had a good talk."

"What did you have to talk about? I mean, Cassion is one of the head guys here. I know he's been teaching you math, but is there something else?"

"Would you be shocked if I told you we talked about the One God. I want to learn more, so I'm planning to go over to the church and talk to the pastor about it after class this afternoon."

He expected Melian's expression to be one of surprise. Instead, she began to smile broadly. "I was aware of your lack of faith. Aunt Zora told me it was because you were never told about the One God. I've been praying for ever so long for you to find and accept Him."

"I guess I have, too. I just didn't know what I was looking for. Like the pastor says, the One God works in mysterious ways."

Chapter Twelve

How time passed so quickly, Chris would never know. His teachers each told him he had surpassed their ability to teach him anything more. With his twenty-first birthday looming on the horizon, Chris did his studying in the library, where he found books on more subjects that interested him. Some of his favorite books were about the ancient history of the world.

"I have some news for you," Hodia said, once she tracked him down in the library. "We've located Marco."

Hearing the name of his childhood friend brought back memories of how he and Marco had lived through the horrors of Henderson Ranch and survived.

"You were right," she continued, "he was working on one of the ranches in southern Mexico. I'd be lying if I told you his living conditions were much better than how the two of you were brought up. It seems the ranch owner is a friend of Mr. Henderson. Most of his hands come to him directly from the ranch. It's a miracle you weren't sent there as well, when you aged out of the program."

"Will he be coming here? Will you be able to help him like you did me?"

"The ranch owner was irate when our people suggested bringing Marco here. It was Marco who made the decision to come with our representative. He should be here early tomorrow morning. When we told him you were with us and was anxious to reunite with him, he broke down in tears. I am afraid you will be sadly disappointed when you see him. He is very undernourished and I've been told he isn't well. If we hadn't found him when we did, he might not have made it."

Chris was terribly saddened by what Hodia told him, but he was excited to be reunited with Marco. He promised himself he would make certain Marco was given the best medical care and education the complex could supply.

~ * ~

Life on the ranch in Mexico was little different from the one Marco lived on Henderson Ranch. He thought he'd gained his freedom when he aged out of the program. It had been Mr. Henderson who took him to the ranch in Mexico and introduced him to Senor Gonzales.

As soon as Mr. Henderson left to return to the states, Marco knew he'd left one hell for another. He longed for the meals he'd eaten all his life when he saw what was being served to the men who were doing the work on the ranch.

He soon recognized boys he'd known all his life. When he confided his displeasure with the conditions, they were quick to warn him. "Do you remember Juan?"

He recalled the boy who was two to three years older than himself and Christopher. He had always been rebellious and one day he was no longer there. No one dared to ask what happened to him, but Marco was certain he had aged out of the program.

"What does he have to do with anything?"

"Henderson sold him to Gonzales, just like he sold the rest of us. We're his slaves. At one time, Juan talked about leaving. The next morning, the foreman came out before we were even out of bed. He forced us to watch as he tied Juan to the whipping post and beat him to death. He told us, 'Let that be a warning to the rest of you'."

Marco felt the wind go out of his sails. Any thoughts of leaving this ranch had been squashed, knowing what happened to Juan. He knew this was going to be his life, no matter how much he hated it.

Over the next several months, his thoughts turned to Christopher. He wondered if he, like himself and the others who were working on the ranch, had been sold to someone as cruel as Gonzales.

He'd just finished working for the day and certainly wasn't looking forward to the evening meal. He knew it would consist of moldy bread and rancid beans. Getting out of the saddle, he saw a strange hover craft in the yard. Before he could ask anyone about them, black spots began to appear before his eyes. It had happened in the past, but this time the spots were becoming larger until entire blackness overcame his entire being.

When he came to, he saw two strangers restraining Gonzales while two others helped him to his feet.

"Are you Marco?" one of the men asked.

He was so weak he could only nod his head in agreement.

"We've been sent here to find you. You're coming with us."

"Y-you can't," he finally managed to say,

"We can and we will. The government has already been alerted to what we have found out here. We have been assured that the military is on its way to arrest Gonzales and rescue the other men who have been working here as slaves for the One God only knows how long."

Marco had no idea what the man meant, but the blackness was again threatening to overcome him. Instead of asking further questions, he merely closed his eyes and allowed his body to give in to the unconsciousness.

~ * ~

Chris hurried to the docking station. It was hard to believe within a matter of minutes he would be reunited with Marco. After what Hodia told him, thoughts of what he might find when he again saw his friend completely overwhelmed him.

Cassion and several members of the medical team joined him in the wait for the hover craft to arrive from Mexico.

In the distance they saw the craft approaching the docking station. The closer it came, the more dread filled Chris's mind. What would he see when at last his friend came off the hover craft?

The first person to enter the area was one of the aliens Chris didn't recognize. "I'm pleased to see you have medical personnel here. I was afraid our passenger might not make it here."

"What do you mean?" Chris asked.

"I've been told Marco is a friend of yours. It might be best if you aren't here when he's brought out of the craft."

Chris could find no words. He shook his head before he finally managed to say, "I'll stay."

Cassion moved closer to his side and comforted him when Marco was carried from the craft on a stretcher. If Chris thought Marco was thin when they were kids, he was now nothing more than skin and bones. How could anyone in this condition have been able to do the ranch work, like they'd done on Henderson Ranch?

"Marco," he whispered hoarsely, "what have they done to you?"

When no response came, Chris realized his friend was unconscious. Even though the medics were running toward the hospital with the gurney, he kept pace with them. There was no way he would leave his friend's side now that he'd been rescued from whatever hell Henderson sent him into.

Why, God? Chris silently prayed. *Why did you bring me here when Marco continued to suffer?*

Although he expected no answer, the voice he now equated with God sounded within his head, followed by the warmth of comfort he'd come to expect. *You were saved to save the others. Together you and Marco will do great things to right the wrongs that have been done for so long.*

~ * ~

It was three days before Marco began to respond positively to the treatments given to save his life. During that time, Chris never left his side. Had it not been for his friends at the complex bringing him meals, he wouldn't have eaten.

"He seems to have turned the corner," Dr. Gratan said late on the third afternoon. "You know it was touch and go for a while, but there is light at the end of the tunnel now. These are doctor's orders, Chris. I want you to go up to your apartment and get some rest. Your presence has been a deciding factor in your friend's recovery. I am certain by this time tomorrow you will see a great improvement in his condition, but not if you don't take care of yourself. I understand how something like this can pray on someone's mind, keeping sleep at bay. Melian is at your apartment waiting for you and she has some medication that I have prescribed so you can get some rest."

The thought of taking medication to sleep didn't sit well with Chris, but he knew if he protested, Melian would call any one of a number of people who would insist he do as he was told.

"I'll be back, Buddy," he whispered, knowing Marco probably couldn't hear him.

Letting go of Marco's hand he got to his feet. After thanking Dr. Gratan, he made his way to the elevator that would take him to the floor where is apartment was located.

As soon as the elevator door opened, he saw Melian standing in the hallway waiting for his arrival.

"I've been so worried about you," she greeted him. "Aunt Zora said you refused to leave your friend's side until you knew he was going to pull through. She said Dr. Gratan gave her some medication for me to give to you. I hope you aren't planning to fight me on this."

"I'm not happy about taking any kind of medication, but Dr. Gratan thinks it's for the best. Will you stay with me until I go to sleep?"

"You know I will."

Once inside the apartment, Melian insisted he get ready for bed and call her once he'd situated himself under the covers.

"Are you sure you want to be a teacher?" he asked when she gave him the medication along with a bottle of water.

"Of course, I am. Why do you ask?"

"Because you would make one bossy nurse."

They both laughed at his statement.

"How is your friend doing?"

"I was horrified when I first saw him. I thought we were thin when we were at the ranch, but the man I saw was nothing more than a skeleton. From what I've been told, Gonzales was working with Henderson to get slave labor for his ranch. Cassion told me the Mexican government is working to relocate everyone who worked on that ranch and has shut down the entire operation. I never understood how Henderson was allowed to do what he did and now to find out Gonzales was perpetuating the horrors is beyond my comprehension."

He wanted to keep talking, but his mind was becoming fuzzy and keeping his eyes open became a monumental task. Before he knew it, the medication sent him into a deep and dreamless sleep.

~ * ~

Marco could feel awareness returning to his body. For some reason, he thought he'd felt Christopher's presence but he knew that was impossible. He didn't even know if Christopher was dead or alive. Had Henderson sold him to another abuser in the same way as he'd done to the men he worked with at Gonzales' ranch? He hoped not, but he wouldn't put anything past Henderson.

He remembered the last conversation he'd had with Christopher. At that time, he'd told his friend about the group run by Patrick Ernst. Had he been able to make it to Idaho, wherever that was, to join up and start a new life? As soon as the memory crossed his mind, he remembered Mr. Henderson as being the one who told him about Patrick Ernst. Had Christopher been sold to Ernst as he had been to Gonzales?

"Marco, can you hear me?"

The voice was that of a man, but he didn't recognize it as anyone from the ranch. With great difficulty, he opened his eyes. Instead of seeing the bunkhouse, he had no idea where he was. The man who was talking to him didn't look at all familiar. Even sitting in the chair beside where Marco slept, it was evident he was very tall, with the most piercing violet-colored eyes he'd ever seen.

"Where am I? Is Gonzales coming to take me back to the ranch? I have work to do and…"

The man in the chair silenced him with a wave of his hand. "You are in a hospital, far away from that hell hole where you have been living.

Gonzales is in the custody of the Mexican government. That's enough for you to know. For now, your job is to get the proper nutrition and regain your strength."

"What about the others?"

"They're being cared for at other facilities."

"Do you know anything about my friend, Christopher?"

"He is the reason you are here. You will see him soon enough and everything will be made clear. I sent him back to his apartment with strict orders that he is to rest. Tomorrow will be soon enough for the two of you to reconnect and have time to talk."

Although he wanted to ask more questions, Marco could feel his strength waning and gave into sleep.

Chapter Thirteen

Chris awoke, more rested than he had been since he first heard about the condition Cassion's agents found Marco in. He was surprised to see Melian sitting beside his bed, as he had for his friend until Dr. Gratan intervened and insisted he return to his apartment to rest.

"Have you been here all night?" he asked.

Melian nodded. "I slept on your sofa. I didn't think you should be alone even though you were heavily sedated. Now that you're awake, I'll contact Aunt Zora and have some food delivered for the two of us."

"I don't have time for that. I have to go to the hospital to be with Marco."

"Not until you eat. Dr. Gratan left strict orders about you having a good meal before you return to the hospital. You don't want to go against doctor's orders, do you?"

"It looks like I don't have much of a choice. If I insist, you'll probably call for reinforcements and force me to do as you say."

"You bet I will," she replied, winking at him broadly.

She went into the living room to wait for their food to be delivered, giving him privacy to shower, shave, and dress in clean clothes.

He no more than exited the bedroom than the alarm alerted him to someone at the door. He crossed the room to wave his hand in front of the pad that controlled the opening of the door.

"Good morning, even though it's afternoon," Zora greeted him. "That medicine Dr. Gratan gave you must have worked miracles. You look completely rested."

She wheeled the car loaded with food into the room. As soon as Chris saw the amount of food, he realized how hungry his forced sleep made him. After removing the cover from each dish, his mouth watered in anticipation of the pancakes, bacon, juice and coffee on the tray.

"This looks like enough for me. What are you going to eat, Melian?" he teased.

"There's more than enough to share," Zora said in response to his statement. "While the two of you eat, I'll fill you in on what's going on at the hospital."

"You have news about Marco?" Chris asked between bites of pancakes and bacon.

"He woke up shortly after Dr. Gratan sent you up here to rest. He's very weak but he did ask about you. Dr. Gratan told him you were here and would be down to see him once you got some rest. We are both certain you have a lot of catching up to do. Mostly the two of you are going to have to steel yourselves for the trial that is certain to be held for both the Hendersons and Gonzales."

Chris could feel a lump forming in his throat. Even though he knew he would eventually be called upon to give testimony against his former caretakers, he prayed there would be enough evidence that he didn't have to take part and face them again.

While Chris ate with great gusto, Melian delicately nibbled at her portion of the food Zora brought for them.

~ * ~

Marco sat up in bed for the first time. It amazed him at how much strength it took to accomplish that one small task.

When his meal was brought to him, he wondered how he would be able to eat. He was still considering how he would get the food from his plate to his mouth when a young woman came to his bedside.

"I'm Kara. Dr. Gratan sent me to help you eat."

"No one's ever fed me, at least not that I remember."

"Nonsense. You are just getting your strength back. I am a nurse here at the hospital and it's my job to help you regain your strength. Until last night we weren't sure if you would ever wake up."

Carefully, she tucked a towel into the neck of the hospital gown he wore and spooned broth into his mouth. It seemed strange to taste the rich broth that was in direct contrast to the swill he'd been eating for most of his life.

Once he finished the broth, she reached for a container. It held some substance he didn't recognize. The first spoonful he tasted was sweet and of a different consistency than the broth. He had no idea what she was feeding him, but he knew he liked it.

"What is this?" he asked.

"Haven't you ever eaten applesauce before?"

He shook his head. "What's it made of?"

The look on her face was one of disbelief. "Don't you know what an apple is?"

He decided his look of bewilderment gave her the answer she wanted.

"Apples are a fruit that grows on trees. Some of the best apples have been cultivated here at the complex. Once they are ripe, they can be eaten raw or cooked with sugar to make applesauce."

Sugar was another word that wasn't in his vocabulary. Growing up, nothing that was served at the ranch was sweet like this wonderful concoction Kara called applesauce.

"If you are able to tolerate these soft foods, Dr. Gratan says you will be ready to start eating regular food soon."

With his hunger satisfied, he appreciated Kara lowering the head of his bed so he could go to sleep. It seemed impossible that he was tired, but everyone assured him it was part of his healing.

~ * ~

Chris finished the last of what he'd put on his plate. Although Melian and Zora were skeptical about him being able to eat so much food, he was determined to prove them wrong. Considering he'd eaten very little since Marco arrived and missed his evening meal the night before, he found he was almost starving. He'd eaten so much that now he was uncomfortable, although he wouldn't let on to the fact that they were right about him not trying to eat too much at one sitting.

"I have to admit, I didn't think you'd be able to eat that much food," Zora said as she cleaned up the dishes.

The alert on her communicator diverted her attention. Although Chris thought it was rude, he listened in on her conversation with Dr. Gratan.

"Are you there with Chris?"

Zora looked up at Chris, indicating that he should join the conversation.

"I'm here," Chris answered.

"That's good. I hope you're rested. Marco is awake and wants to see you."

"I'll be right there."

Without making any other explanation to either Zora or Melian, he hurried out of the apartment to get to the hospital as quickly as possible.

The hospital was buzzing with activity when Chris arrived. He saw Dr. Gratan in the hall before making his way toward Marco's room.

"How's he doing?" he asked.

"Better than I expected. He was awake earlier and took some broth as well as some applesauce. What came as a surprise was when he told the nurse he didn't know what applesauce was."

"It doesn't surprise me. I remember the first time I ate it at Patrick's camp. At the ranch we were never given anything with sugar in it, to say nothing of any fresh fruit. Even though we rarely had either of them at the camp, when we did it was a special treat."

Dr. Gratan nodded his head sagely. "That explains a lot. I wish I would have done a more thorough work up on you when you first arrived. Unfortunately, everyone thought your education was of the upmost importance at the time. Thank goodness you were given a few good meals at the camp. That, in addition to what you've been eating since you arrived here, has kept you in better health than your friend. I fear he is suffering from a severe case of malnutrition."

"Can it be reversed?"

"Yes, but he has a long road ahead of him. For now, he's awake and alert. He's asking to see you. I think you will be some of the best medicine he can have."

Chris made his way to his friend's room. There was much they had to talk about.

As soon as he entered the room, he was overwhelmed by the machines and IV's that were attached to his friend's body.

"Christopher," Marco said, his voice weak and barely audible. "I couldn't believe it when they told me you were here. I thought I dreamed it."

"I met the hover craft when they brought you in. It's a long story, but I'm no longer called Christopher. I shortened it to Chris. I did some research and the English version of your name is Mark. For reasons I'll go into later, I think it's best if you start using it."

A look of confusion crossed Marco's face. "Why do you think this is good?"

"When I made the decision to change my name, it was because I was about to embark on a new life. Christopher, like Marco, was a child. Chris is who I am today, just as you are Mark. It's best to make a complete break with the past."

Mark nodded. "It makes sense. What happened to you after you left the ranch? Did you find Patrick's group?"

"I wanted to ask you about that. How did you hear about them?"

Mark seemed to be tiring.

"We don't have to talk about this now," Chris suggested. "Think about it and we'll talk more after you get some rest. I won't be going anywhere. This is where I live now."

"At the hospital?" Mark asked, as he was slipping off to sleep.

"Not at the hospital. This is a complex built by the Aliens. I know that's something that will need explanation."

He looked down at the bed and realized his friend had heard none of what he'd said. There would be more time in the future for him to explain everything to him and enlist his help when it was time for the trial charging Mr. and Mrs. Henderson with more crimes than he could even comprehend.

~ * ~

When Marco again awoke, he thought about what Chris told him earlier. Changing his name wouldn't erase the past, but he understood the necessity of it. As Marco he would always be reminded of where he came from. Mark would give him a new lease on life. It was what he needed.

Once he was fully aware of his surroundings, he opened his eyes. Chris was sleeping in the chair next to his bed. As much as he wanted to ask the many questions crowding his mind, he was reluctant to interrupt the rest his friend needed.

"Are you awake?"

Chris' question came as a surprise. "I thought you were sleeping."

"Not sleeping, just resting my eyes. Hopefully, you had a good nap."

"I did. I remember you asking me how I knew about Patrick Ernst's group. You did ask me that, didn't you?"

"I didn't think you heard me, but yes, I did ask you that."

"It was Mr. Henderson who told me to tell you about them. He said you weren't cut out to work on any of the ranches in Mexico. He told me you'd do better with a group like his."

"I thought that might be the case. I did join them and I thought it was the best thing I could do. I raised up through the ranks quickly. It wasn't until we came to protest against the aliens here that I realized what we were doing was wrong. We were here with our weapons, ready to fight to the death. I saw two of the recruits who I'd trained killed. Once we came into the complex to meet with their leaders, I was told the truth about the ideals we were fighting for. Suddenly, they didn't seem as important as Patrick told us they were. I also realized the superior race he kept talking about didn't include me. I have Native American blood, just like you come from a Mexican heritage."

"In that group, did they treat you right?"

"They didn't beat me if that's what you mean. The food was a step up from what we got at the ranch. They did feed us three times a day, but only because they needed us to keep up our strength for all the training we did. It wasn't the best food, but at least it wasn't the crap we grew up eating. What I finally realized was that if they'd known about my Native American blood, they would have killed me outright. Thank God, I came here. These people have saved my life. They've also given me the education we were deprived of when we were kids."

"What kind of education?" Mark asked.

"Reading, writing, mathematics, history, geography and science. You have no idea how much it has changed my life."

When Chris looked over, he saw his friend had fallen asleep. It was just as well. Rest was what he needed the most at this point.

Once he was certain Mark was sleeping soundly, he went in search of any information he could find on the raid against the ranch where his friend had been working for the past two years.

He found Cassion in his office and asked if there had been a report written. In response, the older man handed him a tablet. It didn't take long for him to access the document detailing the raid on the ranch in Mexico.

Among the papers that had been seized, was a detailed list of each of the young men who had been 'sold' to Gonzales over the years. Beside each name was a price listed. Reading the names brought back memories of the number of residents who had aged out and disappeared over the years.

There were many names that weren't there and Chris remembered Pops telling him about the young men who he found on the streets before they went on to whatever the future held for them. He wondered how many of them had been sent to groups like the one Patrick headed.

As he thought back, he realized Pops was able to put him in contact with Patrick much too easily. It was possible he knew more about Mr. Henderson than he let on. He didn't want to think of the two of them conspiring to keep the aged-out boys ignorant of the ways of the world. He truly liked both Pops and Ma. For the few days he was in their home, he was treated better than he had in his entire life, until now. Still, there had to be some connection, he just had to figure out what it was.

He realized he'd allowed his mind to wander away from the document he was reading. As he read on, he learned of the punishments that were administered to the young men who worked the ranch when they didn't do exactly what they were told to do.

The further he read, the sicker he became. If he thought the food was bad at Henderson Ranch, it sounded like a banquet compared to what Gonzales was serving. Rather than two meals a day, meals were served only in the evening. It was no wonder Mark was suffering from malnutrition. No one could work as hard as he knew these men were working and be deprived of nourishing meals.

"Are you all right?" Cassion asked.

Chris looked up from the tablet. "Not really. I'm learning more than I ever wanted to know. The way this reads, Mr. Henderson was selling guys like Mark to ranches like the one where you found him."

"Mark?"

"I'm sorry, I told him it would be best if he changed his name from Marco to Mark, the same way I changed mine."

Cassion nodded his head in agreement.

"In my history class, I learned about the slavery that went on in this country until the Civil War. The operation on the Gonzales Ranch sounds like what slavery was in the past. How could something like that happen in the twenty-second century?"

"I tend to agree, but what about you. Why weren't you sent down there?"

"I'm afraid to dig into things more. When Mr. Henderson dropped me off in town, it seems I met the man named Pops too quickly. Also, when I mentioned Patrick Ernst, he was able to contact him immediately. I have a feeling, groups like these are paying Henderson and Pops a bounty for sending them recruits. They hit the jackpot with me, since I learned everything they wanted me to very quickly. It's possible other groups are doing the same thing. If the recruits don't measure up, they disappear."

"Do you really think the man you thought of as your benefactor is in on this as well?"

"I don't know what to think. He was good to me, but things happened far too quickly. It makes me wonder. Do you think someone could look into it?"

"That's a possibility. If we send one of our people they would be spotted immediately, but it's possible Caroline's nephew, Tom, could suggest someone."

Chapter Fourteen

With each passing day, Chris could see Mark's strength returning. Not wanting to put more of a burden on Zora, Hodia, Cassion and Caroline, he enlisted Melian's help in teaching his friend the beginning of reading and mathematics he'd missed learning as a child.

"How could you have learned so much in such a short period of time?" Mark asked.

"I don't know, it just happened. I was talking to Cassion and he has made arrangements for you to have an apartment next to mine. Dr. Gratan says you will be released from the hospital in the next couple of days and you'll need a place to live."

"Apartment?" Mark questioned. "I have no idea what you're talking about."

"I didn't either. You'll have a lot to get used to. I went from living in the dorm to the camp in Idaho. As I see it, you went from the dorm to the bunkhouse on the ranch in Mexico. Having a place all to yourself will take some getting used to. Each apartment has a bedroom, bathroom and living room. There's no need for a kitchen, because we take all of our meals in the dining room."

"Let's change the subject," Mark suggested. "What happened to all the children that were at the ranch?"

Chris cringed at Mark's question. "There was a raid on the ranch and the children were all taken to one of the facilities the aliens have around the country. At least most of them were. They found at least fifteen bodies buried behind the box. They haven't told me if they've found more bodies and I don't think I want to know."

"What has happened to Mr. and Mrs. Henderson?"

"They were arrested and there will be a trial soon. I think they are waiting until more of the children have recovered enough to testify against them. I'm ready whenever the trial is held, but the thought of facing those people again makes me very anxious."

Before Mark could ask any more questions, Hodia entered the room. "I need to talk to you, Chris," she said.

Chris and Mark exchanged glances, each wondering what could be so important to interrupt their time together. She left the room and Chris followed her.

"I have news for you from the people Tom sent to Nevada to check out Paul and Doreen Granger. I hesitate to tell you this, especially since they seemed to befriend you, but we have learned that they were working with Mr. Henderson to supply young men to the militant groups around the country. These groups pay a bounty for each boy they supply. You said the Hendersons gave you money when they dropped you off in town. What happened to it?"

"I've been thinking about that. I know I had a hundred dollars when I went to stay with Pops and Ma, but I didn't have it when I left. When I said something to Patrick about it, he told me I didn't need it and it was more than likely payment for them for taking care of me. Now, I think that might have been Pops' cut for getting us sent to the various groups. It breaks my heart to know they were a part of what went on out at the ranch. I thought they were being good to me."

Unmanly tears prickled behind his eyelids. For all his suspicions, he didn't want any of it to be true. According to what Hodia was telling him, the authorities were being advised to swear out warrants for their arrests. It made him wonder how many people would be involved when all was said and done.

"When will this happen?" he finally managed to ask.

"I'm told they will be arrested later today. I understand you thought these people were your benefactors, but their part in this atrocity the Hendersons and others were carrying out against these children is against the law. I've also heard they have arrested three ranchers in Mexico who were buying boys for slave labor. The web of this horrendous abuse is unraveling at an alarming pace. I'm told the trial for Mr. and Mrs. Henderson will be starting at the beginning of next week.

You are Mark will be taken to Nevada to be witnesses for the prosecution."

"That soon? Do you think Mark is strong enough?"

Hodia took a moment to consider what Chris asked. "I have been talking to the doctors who have been taking care of him and they assure me his progress is nothing short of miraculous. You will both be excellent witnesses. You will also be pleased to see many of the boys who were rescued from the ranch several months ago. They, like you and Mark, have responded both to the medical care they were given and the education they are finally enjoying."

Hodia left him alone in the room where they'd gone to talk. He wished all of this would go away. The thought of testifying against Mr. and Mrs. Henderson, as well as Pops and Ma, terrified him. How could he face his abusers as well as the people who he now knew betrayed him? From what he'd learned in his studies of social practices in the twenty-second century, at the trial, he would be within only a few feet from where he'd be recounting the abuse received for the first eighteen years of his life.

~ * ~

Mark looked much better than he ever remembered him looking in his life when they boarded the hover craft headed for Nevada.

"How do you feel about what we're going to do?" Chris asked.

"I'm excited and frightened at the same time. The last time I saw Mr. Henderson was on my eighteenth birthday when he took me to the Gonzolas ranch in Mexico. I was so excited to be starting a new life. What a farce. The Henderson Ranch was paradise compared to what I found in Mexico. At times I almost wished I could have one of the meals we were fed when we were kids. It would have been ten times better. I can hardly wait for that bastard to come to trial in Mexico. He's one person I will enjoy testifying against."

Mark's response came as a surprise. Chris wondered if his fears of giving testimony against his former abusers were unfounded. He knew in reality it would be for the best. He prayed he would be able bring their reign of terror to an end.

~ * ~

The courthouse in Virginia City, Nevada, was filled to capacity. The press was there, seemingly anxious to see the children and young adults who suffered at the hands of Mr. and Mrs. Henderson.

Chris was surprised when he recognized George and Susan among the crowd. They immediately made their way to his side.

"Uncle George, Aunt Susan, what are you doing here?"

"You're family," George said as he clasped Chris' hand before pulling him into a bear hug. "We couldn't allow you to go through this alone."

"What about your jobs, your families?"

"You might not remember," Susan began, "but George runs his own business, and since it's summer, I have no responsibilities at the school. As for our families, George's wife is taking care of their kids, and my kids are on a camping trip. There is no reason why we shouldn't be here, by your side. Besides, we're hoping we can entice you to come out to our place for a visit when this fiasco is over. We talked to Cassion last night and he thought it would be good for you to get away from the complex for a couple of weeks."

Chris cast a glance toward Mark. How could he abandon his friend, so soon after his rescue from the ranch in Mexico?

"If you're worried about your friend," George said, "he is more than welcome to come along. I think a week or two away from everything will be the best medicine both of you can get."

Before Chris could say anything more, Cassion was at his side. "It's time for the proceedings to begin. You'll need to come to the front of the room and take your seat."

Susan nodded her head and touched his hand before taking her seat at the back of the room. "We'll talk more later."

At the front of the room, he saw that in one row of seats, just behind where he and Mark would be sitting, were about ten of the boys he remembered from the ranch. Each one of them acknowledged them with a nod of their heads.

Even though Chris tried, he was hard put to attach names to these strangers who were sitting behind him. He remembered them as half-starved children. Seeing them now, he realized most of them were young adults, glowing with the health that had been restored since their rescue.

The judge called the proceedings to order and Chris listened as the prosecuting attorney made his opening statement. Listening to the narrative of the atrocities that were performed against all of them for most of their lives made him sick to his stomach. Even though he'd lived it, hearing someone else recounting the charges against the Hendersons, seemed as though he was watching a horror movie.

Chris was the first witness called.

"Mr. Laughlin, how old were you when you went to live on Henderson Ranch?"

"I was about six months old, or so I was told. The first years of my life were good, but the day I turned six, I started riding with the older boys on the ranch."

"Were you fed well?"

Chris swallowed hard. He hated remembering the meals they'd been fed. "Breakfast was a bowl of what they called grits. Sometimes there was milk but more than likely it was sour. Supper was usually some kind of thin soup and dry bread."

"What about the noon meal?"

"There was no noon meal."

"Did you have meat, vegetables?"

"Once a week we were given meat, but it always looked a little green. As for vegetables, I didn't know what they were until I joined Patrick Ernst and his group in Idaho. The meals weren't much better but we did get three meals a day, such as they were."

"Were you punished when you were at Henderson Ranch?"

"I was so hungry, one day I stole a piece of bread from the kitchen. Mrs. Henderson used the paddle on my bottom and Mr. Henderson locked me in the box. I thought I'd been in there for days, but it was only four or five hours. After that I decided I would rather be hungry than locked in that box. I still got hit with the paddle, but I never did anything bad enough to be locked in the box again."

The defense attorney tried to make him out to be a liar, but the truth was the truth. Since coming to the complex and learning about the One God, he knew lying was a sin and one he had no desire to commit.

One by one, Mark and the rest of the boys took the stand and testified to much the same things as Chris told the court. Once they were finished, the aliens who raided the ranch told of the gruesome things they had found when they made the raid. They also testified to the bodies they found buried behind the box.

As soon as the details of what was found were brought into the open, the entire courtroom gasped in disbelief before becoming eerily silent. The only sound were soft sobs from the women who were in attendance.

In their defense, Mr. and Mrs. Henderson told the court what a wonderful thing they were doing by taking these unwanted children into their care. They said they made do with what they were able to get from the state for these undesirables in their care.

The more they defended their position, the sicker Chris became. By the time they finished their testimony, the final arguments were made and the jury were excused to make their decision, Chris got up from his seat and made his way to the rest room. He just made it to the stool when he lost everything he'd eaten from breakfast.

Cold sweat ran down his face as he knelt in front of the toilet, afraid to get up for fear he'd again have to vomit.

"Are you alright?"

He recognized George's voice without turning around. Nodding his head, he got slowly to his feet.

"When I lived it, it was all I ever knew. Hearing the testimony of everyone in there and the weak defense of Mr. and Mrs. Henderson made it all too real. D-do you think they will be found guilty?"

George pulled him into a hug and rubbed his back, as though he was a small child who needed to be comforted. "I'm sure they will. I wish there was still a death penalty in this country. It's what they deserve. From the testimony I heard today, there are at least fifteen charges of murder against them. How anyone could kill innocent children is beyond my understanding. In our culture, children are to be cherished, not treated like dogs and killed."

Chris agreed and allowed his uncle to take him back to the courtroom. They were assured the jury would be out for several hours and that they should take the opportunity to get some lunch. While the other boys were taken away by the people who had brought them there earlier in the day, Mark and Chris accompanied George and Susan to a small restaurant within walking distance of the courthouse.

It came as a surprise when Cassion was there waiting for them to arrive. "You both did well today," Cassion greeted them. "I don't know if I would had been able to testify so confidently, without reaching out to do physical harm to those people."

"I guess the fight went out of me with all the punishments I endured. I'm out of there now and I have a different life. I only want to see justice done. To be truthful, with the correct management, that ranch could be a very profitable business."

"Chris is right," Mark said, joining the conversation. "I know enough about ranching to know a profitable business venture when I see one. They have some good stock out there. I know Mr. Henderson made a good profit by selling his cattle. I wasn't supposed to know that, but I overheard the two of them talking about how much profit they made from selling their beeves as they called them. I'm also willing to bet they didn't eat the same slop they fed us."

"You have a point," Cassion agreed. "Ever since their arrest, our representatives have been taking over the operation. We've been looking for a buyer for the property. I think it would be a good investment for the right person."

Mark nodded. "If I had the money, I'd be interested in taking over the running of the place."

"That's exactly what we wanted to hear," George said.

"What are you talking about, Uncle George?" Chris inquired.

"The elders of our tribe have been talking to Cassion about the disposition of the Henderson Ranch. We aren't ranchers, but with the correct management, it could bring in a good profit."

"Isn't that quite a long way away from Montana?" Chris inquired.

"In this day and age, distance doesn't mean much. It's not like in the old days when we traveled by horse, or even those cars from the twentieth and twenty-first centuries. With the hover crafts we all fly now, it's only a matter of about an hour to get from northern Montana to Nevada. Cassion and I have decided his people would be able to continue working the ranch for us until Mark is able to take over."

Chris broke into a wide grin. "It sounds like your future is secure, Buddy," he said as he reached across the table to clasp Mark's hand. "Now, if I can decide what I want to do with my life, we'd both be set."

"George didn't mean to leave you out of things," Susan added. "We've been doing our research about both of you. Mark is a natural for the ranch life. With the proper education, he will be one of the best managers that we could possibly hire. As for you Chris, I have a feeling that you want more out of life than working on a ranch. Your grades, as well as your ability to learn everything so quickly, means there are so many doors open to you, you'll be able to do anything you want."

"I want to work with kids," Chris admitted.

"I know you do," George replied. "I'm thinking a home for troubled youth would be something that might interest you and…"

"…and the ranch would be perfect for something like that," Mark interrupted. "Between the two of us, we could help troubled kids and run the ranch at the same time."

Chris nodded his head in agreement. If the ranch had had proper management, it could have been the perfect place for kids to live and learn to be the best people they could be.

~ * ~

With the noon meal finished, they returned to the courthouse.

Chris' mind raced with the possibility of what the future held for Mark and himself. At the same time, he didn't know if he ever wanted to return to the ranch that was the subject of so many of his nightmares.

"I just heard that the jury is back with a decision," the prosecuting attorney advised them. "It looks like you got here just in time."

Chris could feel his stomach begin to knot up. He wanted this fiasco to be over. Even so, he worried about what the decision would be. What if the jury decided the Hendersons weren't the monsters he knew them to be?

He took the seat he'd occupied at the beginning of the trial, with Mark sitting next to him. He watched as Mr. and Mrs. Henderson were led back into the courtroom. As they approached the table where they'd sat in the morning to take their seats again, they both turned and glared at Chris and Mark.

"You'll regret this," Mr. Henderson hissed. "Once this farce is over and we're free, you'd better run for your life."

Before the two of them could sit down, the bailiff entered the room. "All rise."

Conversations ceased as the judge came into the courtroom.

Chris watched as the jury filed back into the room. He wished he could read their facial expressions.

"Have you reached a verdict?" the judge asked.

"We have, Your Honor," the foreperson of the jury said, as she passed a folded piece of paper to the bailiff.

It took a moment for the judge to read what was written on the paper. "Is this the unanimous verdict of the jury?"

"It is, your honor."

"Theodor and Celine Henderson, please stand. It is the unanimous verdict of this jury that you are found guilty on all counts of the indictments. Due to the severity of your crimes, I sentence you to life imprisonment on the penal colony on the far side of the moon."

An audible gasp sounded throughout the room as Mrs. Henderson fell to her knees, sobs coming from her lips. "Noooooo! That can't be right. We're innocent I tell you. Innocent. Those boys all lied to you. I know they did."

Chris shook with anger. "How could that woman say such a thing?" he whispered to Mark.

Before Mark could answer, a matron and a male guard entered the room. Electronic cuffs and leg irons were attached to the prisoners' wrists and ankles as they were led out of the room.

"What will their life be like?" Mark asked.

It was Cassion who gave them their answer. "I know that penal colony. My cousin is the warden there. Life for them will not be easy. It was set up for punishments for the hardest of criminals. Considering they are charged with slave trafficking, abuse to minors and fifteen counts of murder, I don't envy them the life they will be living. From what I recall, when they say hard labor, they mean it."

Behind them, the boys who also testified against Mr. and Mrs. Henderson, were jubilant in their reaction to the verdict handed down by the judge and jury.

Chapter Fifteen

Rather than return to the complex, Chris returned to Montana with George and Susan. He had no idea what he would find when he arrived at the reservation. Many of the history books Caroline had given him to read described the reservations where the Native Americans were living as substandard as the living conditions on Henderson Ranch.

He was pleasantly surprised to see George land his hover craft in front of a well-maintained home.

"It's not what you were expecting," George said. "When we were at the complex, I took some time to talk to Caroline. She said she was teaching you history, especially the history of our people. Since her memories are over a hundred years old, I'm certain you thought you would find us living in squalor. A lot of things have changed in the twenty-second century. Our people have come a long way since the aliens came."

Chris nodded. This certainly wasn't what he expected, although he should have known better considering what George said about the tribe buying the Henderson Ranch.

"Do you have any idea why the white side of my family wasn't at the trial?"

George turned to face Chris. The expression on his face was one of indecision. "They were contacted, the same as we were. I'm told they said your grandmother was not feeling well and wouldn't be able to make the trip. I think Marie wanted to come, but Chester is something else."

"That's what I thought," Chris said. "The impression I got when I first met him was that he wanted nothing to do with me. My grandmother said it was because my father was smart and didn't want to go into the company business. I couldn't understand it. The way he acted when we first met, made me think he thought I was going to ask him for something other than family heritage. I feel bad for the fact that my grandmother wants me in her life, but I doubt Uncle Chester would ever allow it."

"I worry about her as well. I was thinking of getting in contact with her and seeing if she and your Aunt Marie would like to come out here while you're visiting. That is, if you would be agreeable to the suggestion."

Chris didn't know what to say. He wanted to reconnect with the paternal side of his family, but he worried about Uncle Chester. Would he interfere with any plans for a reunion?

"If they would like to come here, I would appreciate it. Still, I don't want to drive a wedge between them and my uncle. My grandmother lost one son, I don't think she's strong enough to lose another, even though it isn't through death. I have a feeling he is a hard man."

"I think you're right, but we should give your grandmother and Marie the opportunity to make up their own minds."

Chris agreed, but knew this wasn't the time to make the decision. The trial had been draining, to say the very least. What he wanted most was to rest.

~ * ~

The next morning, George suggested they make contact with Marie to see how she felt about coming out to the reservation to meet with them.

"I know Chester was evasive when you called him earlier about coming out to Nevada for the trial. I think he could have been more forthcoming, but we were both quite upset, not about the trial mind you. Our mother suffered a stroke after we were at the compound to meet with Chris. Thank goodness we caught it early and the doctors were able to reverse the effects of it. Let me talk to Chester and Mom and get back to you. I know Mom will be thrilled about making the trip, and I can get away without a problem, at least for a few days. Chester, on the other hand, might have more problems with it. He and his son have been running the business, but the boy wanted to go to college, and it left my brother holding the bag, so to speak. I'll contact you later today and let you know what plans we're making."

The connection on the communicator went dark, leaving Chris to think about the cousin who might be more like him and the man who fathered him, than his own father. From the original meeting he'd endured with Chester, he came to the conclusion his uncle was not a highly educated man. If he wasn't thrilled about his brother's quest for an education, how would he feel about the same trait in his son?

Less than an hour later, George's communicator lit up, showing not only Marie but also Felicia's face.

"Is Chris there with you?" Marie asked.

"Yes, I'm here," Chris said, looking directly into the camera.

"It's so good to see you," Felicia exclaimed. "We have checked with my doctors and they have told me it will be safe for me to travel, only not commercially. Marie and I are making plans to leave for there early tomorrow morning. It won't be as fast as a commercial flight, but her hover craft will get us there by midafternoon."

"Are you certain it will be safe?" George asked.

"Perfectly. Thanks to the quick actions of Marie and her husband, I was able to get treated immediately and have all of my functions returned. Besides, my doctor thinks a change of scenery and getting to see my grandson will be the best medicine I can get."

Chris could see tears in his grandmother's eyes and knew how much she loved him. Turning away from the screen, he listened as George gave Marie detailed directions to his Montana home.

"What about Chester?" he heard George ask.

"He wanted to come with us, but he won't be able to get away until the weekend. He said he would be flying out, commercially, on Friday. The plant runs a four ten-hour day shift so he has the entire three-day weekend. I know Chris thinks Chester is cold, but it takes him a while to come around to new ideas. We were talking about everything at the time of the trail. Even though we weren't able to make it because of Mom's stroke, he followed the proceedings online. I have a feeling if those monsters hadn't been sent to that penal colony, he would have come out there and killed them. Thank goodness justice was served and we were able to come to grips with what they'd done to so many children. Thank God, there will be no more children sent into that situation in the future."

Chris could hardly believe his ears when he heard Marie tell of the anger Chester displayed during the trial, even though he couldn't be at the trial to stand by Chris' side. It was possible he'd completely misjudged the man.

~ * ~

It was just a little after three the next afternoon when Marie and Felicia arrived at George's home. While Chris worried about the burden his Illinois family would put on George and Susan, he shouldn't have. It seemed as though there was always space for two or three more at the table and extra rooms didn't seem to be a problem either.

Chris was surprised when Marie brought her husband, Frank, with them. She also made the announcement they'd located a bed and breakfast where the two of them could stay and enjoy what she called a second honeymoon. She also said Chester and his wife Wanda would be staying at the same facility. Since it was within walking distance to George's home.

Although George's wife, Nancy, was disappointed not to have Susan and Frank staying with them, she understood their need for privacy.

"I've been making plans, myself," Robert Crow, Susan's husband announced. "Since Chester and his wife, Wanda, are coming I think it's time your entire family gets in touch with this side of your heritage. With George and I both being members of the tribal elders, we arranged for an impromptu pow-wow. There will be dancing and traditional food as well as some of our best tribal singers."

Marie clapped her hands like an excited child. "Remember when you and Dad used to take us down to Peoria for the pow-wows at the Wildlife Prairie Park, Mom? As I recall, Carter and Chester both declared they wanted to be Indians when they grew up."

"I've heard about that pow-wow," George replied. "As I recall, our folks wanted to go, but the timing was never right. They were ranchers and spring was always a bad time of year to be away from home."

Chris took an immediate interest in the conversation. "What happened to the ranch?" he finally asked.

"I hated ranching and wanted to pursue other things. Dad finally sold it and retired. I think that was the beginning of the end for him. His health declined and he passed away about a year after he retired. Mom followed him, within six months. I think she died of a broken heart. Not only had she lost her husband, but her oldest child disappeared without a trace almost fifteen years earlier."

For the first time, Chris wondered about what George did for a living. How had he been able to come to not only the complex but also to the trial? Didn't he have to work?

"What do you do for a living, Uncle George?" Chris blurted out.

"I wondered how long it would take you to ask. I'm the accountant for our tribe. There's no reason to rent office space, when I can work on my own time from home. My schedule is quite flexible, unlike Susan's. She has to work around her teaching both in the classroom and virtually. Back a hundred years ago, no one knew much about virtual learning, but when that damn pandemic hit, everything changed."

"To be truthful, the virtual classroom was a great boon to our reservation. There are so many outlying ranches, it used to be hard to get all of the kids into town for school. Now my in-person classroom and our virtual one work perfectly for everyone. We've come a long way from the days when the kids on the reservation were shipped off to the government run boarding schools to turn them into little white kids. Today our children are taught not only the basics required by the government, but also the proud history of our people."

Marie was smiling broadly. "It sounds like you do great work, Susan. In case you're interested, Frank and I also do a lot of work virtually. We're interior designers and do a lot of our work on the computer. It's one reason I'm able to travel at the drop of hat because we can be in contact with our clients from anywhere in the world."

Felica smiled. "It seems like all of you children have made a mark in this world. I think Carter would have been proud of all of your accomplishments. I often wonder what he would have done with his life. The closest I can come is going to be watching Chris bloom into the productive adult his father would have been."

Chris sat, listening to his grandmother and aunt talking about their lives. He thought about how different his life might have been if there hadn't been an accident that took the lives of both of his parents.

I will make you proud, Mom and Dad. With the old Henderson Ranch being purchased and Mark running it. Maybe that is where his future belongs. It's possible there might be something he can do and maybe I can help with, to turn it from being a hell hole to being a sanctuary for children without families.

For a moment, only his thoughts resonated through his mind. He certainly didn't expect the answer that came suddenly from the voice he now recognized as belonging to his father.

You and Mark will do great things there, but in the future, there will be no unwanted children. Instead, it will become a working ranch as well as a summer camp for kids. I predict that in the winter, there will be young adults who will flock there to learn the skills of ranching and for higher education. Between the two of you, as well as the aliens who will be there to help you, it will become a bright spot in education.

Chris shook his head. Had he actually heard the voice of his dead father? He was certain he had, but his prediction made no sense. He had no idea what he wanted to do with his life, but the last place on earth he wanted to be was back at the Henderson Ranch.

~ * ~

At the beginning of the weekend, Chester and his wife, Wanda, arrived at the reservation. While George and Susan seemed to be thrilled with the new arrivals, Chris still had concerns about meeting his last aunt.

Like Chester, Wanda didn't seem to be comfortable in George's modest home. It was evident that she was used to a life of luxury. Unlike Susan, Marie and his grandmother, she wore heavy makeup.

Chris had only seen pictures of such painted ladies, as he liked to call them, in some of the books he read while he was at the compound. None of the other women he'd met, since being rescued from the life he'd lived for the first twenty years of his life, wore such outrageous cosmetics on their faces. Seeing Aunt Wanda made him appreciate the natural beauty of the other women who had entered his life over the past few months.

"This is a lovely home," Wanda said, her voice dipping with sarcasm. "You've done so much with it. I'm surprised to find a home like this on the reservation. From what I've read your people have lived in poverty for many generations."

Chester looked mortified by her comment.

"That's ancient history," Susan informed her. "Since the race riots of the twenty-first century, things have changed for many people of color. The government put in practices set forth when our forefathers established this country. In other words, Liberty and Justice for All."

Chris decided it was best if he kept his mouth shut. Because he was of mixed race, he'd been sent to Henderson Ranch when he was just a six-month-old baby. How could that be liberty or justice? He'd been little more than a slave for the first eighteen years of his life, and a follower of a charismatic leader for the next two. He hadn't found either liberty or justice until he went to live at the compound. It was there he first learned the meaning of the words unconditional love.

"When we met at the compound," Chester said, breaking into Chris' thoughts, "you mentioned working with children. Have you changed your mind? I never went to college, but I had a lot of friends that did, and they changed their minds many times before they found exactly what they wanted to do with their lives."

"At this point in my life, I still plan to work with kids, but like you said, I could change my mind many times. I still have a lot of schooling ahead of me. There's still the trial for Pops and Ma to be held. I saw them as my saviors, but in fact they were as much involved in the business of selling children as the Hendersons were. True, they weren't as cruel as the Hendersons, but they profited from selling kids not only to people like

Patrick Ernst, but also to the ranches in Mexico, where people like my friend Mark traded one cruel master for another. Until all of the trials are finished, I can't think about looking to the future."

"Well said," George commented, slapping Chris on the back. "The future is unlimited. What you must concentrate on is the here and now."

The here and now, George's words resonated in Chris' mind. *What is the here and now? I feel like I'm in limbo, until my future life is revealed to me. It's just too much to contemplate at this stage in my life.*

Chapter Sixteen

All too soon, Chris' visit with both sides of his family came to an end. He was surprised at how his opinion of Chester changed over a matter of a few days. The man he originally thought was cold and unfeeling turned out to be someone who was simply hard to get to know. Once he got to know Chester, Chris realized this was his father's full brother, the closest he would ever come to getting to know the man who gave him life.

It came as a surprise when he found he actually felt lonely and was missing his family. It was amazing how these strangers could have become so important to him in such a short amount of time.

"Welcome home, Buddy," Mark greeted him, when he entered the dining hall. "It certainly seemed strange to come back here without you."

"Something tells me you probably weren't all that lonely with Kara in your life."

Mark's eyes twinkled with merriment at the mention of the nurse who had taken care of him when he first arrived at the compound.

"I have been seeing Kara, but only when she has free time. She's kept very busy at the hospital. While we were gone, two of the younger kids from the ranch were transferred here. It seems that the facility where they were taken was not able to give them the specialized care that they needed for the malnutrition they suffered from. I'm told they were in a lot worse shape than we ever were. I've met with them but I don't remember them from my time there. From the things they told the doctors, things got a lot worse after the two of us left."

Chris felt his heart break. Things at the ranch had been rough when he was a kid. How could they have gotten worse in the three years since he left?

"What do you think about the offer from Uncle George's tribe to buy the ranch?"

"I'm excited about the idea of turning the ranch into a working ranch and a sanctuary for children. Still, I have a lot of education to finish before I will be ready for anything like that. I did talk with Cassion about it, and he thinks it's a great idea. He's working on a plan where some of his people will come along with me when I'm ready to return there. He wants to establish a proper school, as well as a medical facility and good housing. My education will continue while I oversee the running of the ranch. Let's face it, Chris, ranching is the only thing I know, and to be truthful, I'm good at it. The whole thing excites me. What about you?"

"I don't know what I want to do with my life. We did a lot of talking about it while I was with both sides of my family this week. They all agree that I could probably change my mind several times over the next few weeks, months and years. I want to work with children, but at this point, I don't know if I could ever return to the ranch. If I tell you something, I hope you won't think I'm crazy."

"Like, how could I think that? We're friends, have been for most of our lives. What do you want to tell me?"

Chris took a deep breath. "I think I've been hearing my father's voice in my mind. It all started when I dreamed about him and my mother. Now I hear him when I'm trying to make a decision. He told me that the two of us are going to do great things at the ranch. I'm not so sure about that, but he says, in the future we will see the ranch become a place for higher learning as well as a working ranch."

Mark looked as though he was contemplating the idea Chris put forth. "It's certainly something to think about. I have a feeling it's a long way off in the future, but it could be possible, with a lot of hard work. Hopefully, Cassion and his people will still be willing to help out when I'm prepared to return there."

Before they could continue, Melian and Kara joined them.

"I missed you," Melian said as she sat down next to Chris. "When did you get back?"

Chris realized how much he'd missed seeing Melian and cursed himself for not going to see her as soon as he arrived back at the complex.

"It was late last night. I was certain you were probably already in bed. It was an exhausting visit and return flight back here."

"How did you get along with your family?"

"Better than I thought. I knew I would get along well with my mother's family. My concerns were for the family of my father. I saw a completely different side of Uncle Chester than I did when he was here. I also met his wife, Wanda, and Marie's husband, Frank. I didn't warm up to Aunt Wanda at first. She wore a lot of face makeup. I was very surprised by it, because no one here wears it. I actually thought she was a snob, but underneath the makeup and her outward feelings about people, I learned she's actually a nice person. Can you tell me why some women wear so much face makeup?"

"I think I can answer that," Kara said. "I've done a lot of research about the beauty practices of the women who are native to earth. Face makeup has been touted as enhancers to beauty since the beginning of time. To be truthful, some of the women from our colony on the dark side of the moon use makeup or cosmetics as they call them. They think they make them more beautiful. I've tried them, but it takes too much time for my liking. If people don't like the way I look naturally, I don't care. This is how I was brought up by my parents, and how I believe I want to live my life."

Chris nodded. He agreed with Kara. He could see no value in the makeup his Aunt Wanda used so liberally. It was a certainty that she would have been much more beautiful without the makeup she put on her face.

~ * ~

Chris was surprised when he went to his morning class. He expected to see Caroline, instead, Hodia was his teacher for the day.

"Is something wrong with Caroline?" he asked before taking his seat.

"Nothing wrong, necessarily, she is close to the time when she is due to deliver her baby and Dr. Aragon has insisted that she should be taking more time to rest."

Chris nodded. He knew little about the process of childbirth, but he did know that Caroline, as an older woman, was at a higher risk than a younger woman in the same position would be.

"How long will it be before she will have the baby?"

"Only the baby and the One God knows the answer to your question. Babies come on their own schedule, but Dr. Aragon thinks it could be some time before the end of this week. Perhaps today's lesson should be on biology and what transpires between a man and a woman."

He didn't know how he felt about her suggestion. When he was a teenager, Theodore Henderson told him and the other boys his age that sex was a dirty disgusting thing, and it was something best left alone. He told them all women were whores and they wanted only to lead young men astray with the promise of sex.

"I-I don't know about that," Chris stammered. "Isn't sex something dirty?"

"Hardly. The One God created man and woman. Sex, as you call it, should be an act of love. It is meant to be engaged in by committed couples who love each other and want to give each other pleasure. Sometimes it results in the making of a new life. Your parents, my parents, and the parents of everyone here, made love, and we were the product of that love. Did you learn about the love your parents shared when you were with your family these past days?"

Chris nodded his head. "Uncle George and Aunt Susan both told me how much my mother loved my father. Even though their actions were not to the standards of her family, they were planning a life together. They wanted to be married and form their own family."

Hodia smiled at his statement. "What about your father's family? How did they feel?"

"Uncle Chester said he'd received a letter from my father saying he'd met someone he wanted to spend the rest of his life with. What they did before marriage wasn't what either family approved of, but from everything I learned, they were very much in love with each other. Had they lived; I think we would have been a happy family."

"I agree with you. For today, let's see if we can change the things you learned at Henderson Ranch. Before we begin, I'm going to have Mark brought to our classroom. What we need to cover is something he should be learning as well. I'm told he is developing feelings for Kara. It's not that I disapprove of such a relationship, as I also don't disapprove of your feelings for Melian. I do believe it's best if both of you know more about biology and the act of making love."

It took only a few minutes for Mark to join them for the morning session of their schooling. Together they listened as Hodia explained the information that was brought up on their tablets.

Chris knew he would be delving deeper into the information he'd been given. Everything she said was in direct contrast to what the Hendersons had told them throughout their young lives.

~ * ~

By the time they broke for lunch, Chris and Mark had many more things to consider than they did prior to the class on biology.

Although Melian joined them, Kara was not there.

"I thought I'd see Kara," Mark lamented.

"She's tied up at the hospital," Melian replied. "I've been told that Caroline has gone into labor and Kara has been assigned to be her nurse until it's the time for the delivery of her baby."

Chris relived much of the information given him this morning in class. Hodia talked about how babies were conceived and the pain as well as the agony a woman went through when she gave birth. From what he'd learned, his mother had no such experience, as he had been surgically removed from her body just prior to her death. Had she been anxiously awaiting his birth? Did she feel him move within the confines of her body? Would she have welcomed the pain of childbirth?

Oh, my dear Chris, I felt every movement you made. I loved you from the first moment I realized you were growing inside me. Even as my physical life was slipping away, I saw you being born and prayed to the One God you would have a good life. I am so sorry for what the first twenty years of life were like for you. Thanks to the One God and the people at the complex for the chance you are being given to live the life that you deserve. Believe that I loved you before you were you and I love you even more today.

Chris was becoming more comfortable hearing the voices of his departed parents within the confines of his mind. Each time it happened, it came as a surprise, but the advice they gave him proved to be worth listening to and following.

"Are you with us?" Mark asked, bringing Chris back from the voice of his mother that was sounding in his mind.

"I am."

"I have a feeling you were communicating with your father again."

"No, it was my mother. She said, even as she was dying, she saw my birth. From what I've been reading of the information I got from the church, there is such a thing as life after death. If they weren't together with the One God, how could they be communicating with me?"

"You are beginning to understand," Melian exclaimed. "What you are learning is what I've been taught for my entire life. I can't even begin to imagine not knowing the love of the One God and the promise He gives for eternal life."

"It's a learning process, but I'm getting there. How about you Mark, have you had a chance to go to the services at the church?"

Mark nodded. "Kara is a firm believer and has been helping me come to grips with not only everything that is happening in my life, but also the idea of the One God. I plan to talk to the pastor soon. She tells me that he will be able to answer many more of my questions than she can."

They ate the rest of their noon meal in silence, each contemplating the things they'd been learning over the past days and weeks.

The dining room was beginning to clear out when Kara entered the area. "Caroline has a healthy baby boy," she declared.

Applause broke out from everyone in the area.

"Why all the excitement?" Mark questioned. "After what Hodia taught us today, I thought this was a very natural happening."

Kara smiled, as she seated herself at their table. "Normally it is, but Caroline is a very special new mother. She lived over one hundred years ago. At that time, she went into suspended animation and wasn't awakened until recently. In effect, she is a normal forty-three-year-old woman who is perfectly capable of having a child. Since no Earthling has ever been brought back to life after so long, to say nothing of getting pregnant and giving birth, it is quite a miraculous event."

Chris realized, although he knew about Caroline's circumstances, Mark had no idea of what the older woman had been through in her lifetime.

"I met Caroline when I first came to the complex," Chris said, in an attempt to explain the situation. "She told me all about her past and taught me about a lot of history that somehow has been forgotten, or in other words, is no longer taught in the schools. The President referred to her as a National Treasure. I'm pleased to be able to call her my friend."

"Wow, that's quite a story. I can hardly wait until I can meet this woman. Do you think she will be one of my teachers?"

Chris looked to Melian and Kara for an answer.

"Having a baby is draining for even a young woman," Melian replied. "At her age, she will have to take a while longer to regain her strength. We are blessed that Zora has been studying under her, so she can take over your lessons. I'm sure Caroline and her husband, Aaron, will be anxious to show off their newest arrival. Do you know what they are going to name him?"

Kara was quick to respond. "They are going to name him Johnathan Adam, for Caroline's brother and first husband. He is a good-sized baby. He weighed seven pounds nine ounces and is twenty-one inches long. He's already been chipped with his DNA and they will be able to return to their apartment sometime either tomorrow or the next day."

Chris marveled at how quickly things like this happened. From what he'd learned from Dr. Parker, it had been six months before he was able to leave the hospital. Of course, he had been born far too early, where little Johnathan came at the time he was expected. He was certain if he delved more deeply in the biology information on his tablet, he would learn all about how these things happened.

~ * ~

While Chris went to his history class, Mark continued on to another classroom where he would be learning the elementary things Chris had breezed through previously. He prayed his friend would learn as quickly as he had.

Zora proved to be as knowledgeable as Caroline had been, and made the history of, not only the people of Earth, but those who had bases under the Antarctica and on the dark side of the moon as well, come to life.

What she dwelled on today was of how the Aliens watched as the pioneers made their way across the vast expanse of what is now the United States of America. Reading about the hardy people who made the trip, he also learned of the Native Americans, who were forced to fight for the land that had been theirs since the beginning of time.

Although he admired the people who made the grueling trip west, he also identified with the people, who like his mother's family, were the original inhabitants of the land. The account he read called them Indians and savages. It was evident, they were so much more. They had families, lived in communities, and worshiped the gods of their people. The more he read, he decided they were no different from the people who were forcing them off their land. They lived and loved in the same way and their blood ran just as red as that of the intruders.

He could feel the anguish of the people on both sides who lost friends and family in the fighting to control the land that spread in front of them.

As he finished reading the assigned material, he found unmanly tears running down his cheeks. He cried for the people from families like the one his father left behind, as well as those who were the ancestors of his mother's people. Never before had he felt so moved by reading or even hearing a story. To him these were stories, but they were also the history of both sides of his family.

Chapter Seventeen

Life fell into a predictable pattern of classes, not only of academic value, but also spiritual ones from Chris' meeting with the pastor at the church.

He was surprised when Cassion joined him while he was eating the morning meal. "Is something wrong?" Chris asked.

"Not wrong. I wanted to tell you the trial for the Grangers, Pops and Ma, will be starting next week. The judge has asked that you be present. I know you think they were your saviors, but from what we've learned they were working in tandem with the Hendersons. Your testimony will be very beneficial."

"I honestly don't know how I feel about being in the same room with them, even though I knew this day was coming. They gave me good food and a soft bed. I thought it was paradise compared with what I experienced for the first eighteen years of my life. I didn't think anything about the money the Hendersons gave me until I was on my way to Patrick's camp. I believed him when he said Ma would look for it and send it on to me. I was learning so much while I was at the camp, I completely forgot about it. At that point in time, I had no idea about the meaning of money. Mr. Henderson told me it was something I would need since the ranch was not going to be providing for all my needs."

"It makes sense that either Paul or Doreen Granger took the money. I'm certain it supplements what money he makes at his job. It's also possible that Ernst pays a premium for any recruits the Granger's send his way. I've also learned that even though Mark was taken to Mexico by Mr. Henderson, Paul Granger also takes young men from the ranch down to other ranches in Mexico."

Chris cradled his head in his hands for a moment. "That's a lot to digest. To be truthful, it turns my stomach, but I know this is something I need to do. When do we leave for Nevada?"

"We will be leaving in the morning. I've made arrangements with all of your classes. The information you will be needing to continue your studies has been downloaded to your tablet, so when you aren't at the courthouse, you can keep up with your assignments."

Chris thought back to when he and Mark went to that same courthouse for the trial for the Hendersons. At that time Mark hadn't begun his formal education and Chris was assured he had completed enough of his classes that he deserved a break to spend time with his family. This trip would be entirely different. Mark wouldn't be going with him. He would be on his own, and in addition to his testimony at the trial, he would be expected to keep up with his studies. He prayed he could keep his mind on what he was supposed to learn in the midst of the emotional trial.

~ * ~

The courtroom, although familiar, had a different air about it. Instead of the several young boys who testified against the Hendersons, the seats in the front row were occupied by young men Chris recognized as being with him at the ranch.

"Christopher, is that you?" A young man Chris recognized as Peter, although he couldn't remember his last name, asked.

"It's Chris now," he replied. "Where have you been since you left the ranch?"

He knew he didn't have to ask the question. Peter's gaunt appearance reminded him of Mark when he was first brought to the complex. It was evident he had been working on one of the ranches in Mexico. His skin was leathery brown from the amount of time he spent in the sun and he was definitely suffering from malnutrition.

"After I left the ranch, Mr. Henderson gave me a hundred dollars and took me into town. Before I knew it, Pops came up to me and took me home with him. I thought the nightmare was over, but it was only just beginning. The next morning, Pops took me to a ranch in Mexico. When we arrived, the rancher came and put shackles on my ankles. He paid Pops some money and took me with him. If you thought the Henderson's ranch was bad, it was nothing compared to the one in Mexico. We were chained to our beds at night so that we wouldn't run away, and the overseers made certain we did our work during the day. I couldn't believe it when they raided the ranch and took us to the Alien complex just outside of Mexico City. When they told me that it was all because of you, I couldn't believe it. I don't know how I could ever repay you."

"There's no repayment needed," Chris informed his former friend. "Are they treating you well at the complex?"

"I've only been there for about a week, but they have been giving me good medical treatment, the best food I've ever eaten and they tell me they're going to give me the education I was denied as a child."

"That's good. They're doing the same for me and for Marco, although now he's called Mark. I've actually found both sides of my family and the people on my mother's side are buying the ranch. They want to turn it into a school for the children who were taken from there and they want Mark to manage it for them."

"What happened to the Hendersons?"

Chris swallowed down the gall that came into his throat at the thought of the trial he'd attended months earlier. "They were tried in this very courthouse and sentenced to life imprisonment in a penal colony on the dark side of the moon."

Saying the words brought immediate satisfaction. He was able to assure Peter that never again would the Hendersons be able to harm any more children.

Their conversation came to an end when Paul and Doreen Granger were brought into the courtroom. They each wore a nondescript orange jumpsuit with shackles on their ankles and hands.

"All rise," the bailiff announced. "This court is now in session. The Honorable Phillip Armstrong presiding."

Chris and Peter both got to their feet and stood, until they were instructed to return to their seats. If nothing else had been learned at Henderson Ranch, it was obedience.

The prosecution presented their case and called several young men to the stand. Each of them told the same story as what Peter told Chris earlier.

At last, it was Chris' turn to take the stand.

"Please state your name," the prosecutor ordered.

"Christopher Laughlin," he replied.

"How do you know the defendants, Paul and Doreen Granger?"

Chris related the way Paul, aka Pops, approached him on the street and insisted he come to their home. When he mentioned Patrick Ernst, Pops had been able to contact the man almost immediately.

"How did you hear about Patrick Ernst?"

"My friend, Mark, said he'd heard about how Patrick was giving men like me a place to stay. I learned later that Mr. Henderson told Mark to tell me that. I wasn't very good at ranching, and he thought if I were sent to Ernst's group, I would, more than likely, be killed because of my mixed blood. I was lucky that they never found out about my heritage until we made the raid on the complex of the Aliens in Denver. Once I told them of my background, I knew I would no longer be welcomed in their group. I was blessed when the Aliens allowed me to stay and receive the education that I'd been denied at Henderson Ranch."

"How were you treated in the Granger home?" the defense attorney asked in his cross examination.

"For the first time I had a good meal and a soft bed."

"If they treated you so well, why are you testifying against them?"

"When I went there, I had a hundred dollars that Mr. Henderson gave me. When I left, I no longer had the money. I didn't see the money change hands, but I heard enough while I was with Patrick's group to understand that he paid people like the Grangers to supply him with recruits for his militant group. At one time, Patrick told me I was his, bought and paid for. It wasn't the torture that the guys who were sent to Mexico endured, but it was bad enough."

"Bad enough, how?" the defense attorney pressed.

Chris continued to tell of the living conditions as well as the poor food they were given, while living with the skinheads.

It was almost noon when Chris finished his testimony and the court recessed for the midday meal. He was immediately met by Cassion.

"I've made reservations for us at a small restaurant just down the street."

Chris glanced back at Peter and saw his friend being escorted from the courthouse by a man who could only be an Alien from the complex by Mexico City. With him were several other young men who testified earlier to the same things as what Peter told the court.

"Do you think we should ask them to eat with us?" Chris asked.

"Not this time. There are some things the two of us need to talk about."

Chris silently questioned Cassion's statement.

Once they were seated at the table and their order was taken, Cassion elaborated on what he said earlier.

"This afternoon, the Grangers will be taking the stand in their own defense. I want you to be ready for whatever they have to say. In your testimony, you were the one who mentioned Ernst's group to them. Was there a reason for that?"

"Mark told me about the group. He said Mr. Henderson told him he thought I would be better suited to join up with them than to work in Mexico. As I recall, Mark was looking forward to going to one of the Mexican ranches. That was mostly because he knew the language and I didn't."

"Why did they teach Mark Spanish and not you?"

"Mark was older when he came to the ranch. His mother had been Mexican and he was fluent in Spanish when he came. Thinking back on it, I resented the fact he could speak a language I didn't understand. Mr. Henderson and one of the hired men spoke Spanish to Mark all the time. I always thought it was because they didn't want me to understand what they were saying. Now I know they were grooming Mark for the life he was destined to live on the ranch in Mexico."

"When you mentioned Ernst's group, did Pops seem to be surprised."

"No. He was able to contact Patrick almost immediately."

"Hmm, I think I understand. Let's see what the Granger's have to say this afternoon. You might be recalled to the stand as a rebuttal witness."

Chris wasn't comfortable enough with the legal system to completely understand what Cassion was talking about. It didn't matter what his mentor meant. He knew he would have to do whatever it took for the Grangers to be brought to justice.

~ * ~

The afternoon session was about to be called to order when the Grangers were brought back into the courtroom. To say Chris was shocked by what he saw was a complete understatement.

Doreen Granger, who had walked in with her head held high just hours earlier, now leaned heavily on a cane. It was also evident she was wearing heavy makeup that made her look much older than she had for the morning session.

The first person called to the stand was Doreen.

"Mrs. Granger, were you and your husband collaborating with Theodore Henderson to sell the boys from Henderson Ranch to groups like the Mexican ranchers and Patrick Ernst?"

Her reply was hardly more than a harsh whisper. "Paul would often bring home young men he met on the street. He called it his Christian mission in life. I would give them a good meal, a hot bath and a clean bed. Once they left, I had no idea where they went or what happened to them."

From the first row of the courthouse, there was an audible gasp.

"She's lying," Chris whispered to Cassion.

"I know. Before we took our seats, I talked to the prosecuting attorney. It's something we were expecting."

Chris took a cleansing breath before looking to his left at Peter and the other young men who testified earlier in the day. He could see the same thoughts about the lies Doreen was telling as what he was harboring.

Rather than concentrate on his internal thoughts, Chris turned his mind to the cross examination of Doreen.

"You say you had no idea of what happened to the young men after they left your home, but the testimony this morning tends to tell a different story. What do you have to say about that?"

Doreen licked her lips, and stared directly at the men in the front row who had been called to the stand earlier in the day.

"You know how young men like to embellish stories. It's not my fault they are all ignorant in the ways of the world. They like to make things look like something they aren't. We did nothing but give them a place to stay when they seemed to be lost and alone."

"Each of the men said they were given money when they left the Henderson Ranch. They also said when they left your home the money was missing. Do you have any idea what happened to their money?"

"What do those bastards know about money? They probably squandered it long before they ever arrived at our house. They were nothing more than ignorant misfits. You can't give money to stupid people and hope to have them know what to do with it."

Chris couldn't believe what he was hearing. He remembered the money he had when he arrived at the Granger home. Thinking back on it, he recalled putting the stash of five twenty-dollar bills, into the dresser drawer when he went to bed for the night. He'd been so tired and the bed was so soft, it was possible someone could have come into the room and taken the money while he slept.

Tears of grief flowed down his cheeks. He wasn't ashamed of them. Instead, his shame was reserved for the two people who had treated him with respect for the first time in his life. They were no better than Theodore and Celine Henderson. They just disguised their motives. Not only did they steal the money he'd been given, but they had also sold him, as well as many others, into lives that were not much different from the way they'd been treated throughout their childhood.

Doreen left the stand and leaned heavily on her attorney as he helped her to go back to the seat where she'd sat for the entire morning.

Try as he might, Chris could feel no sympathy for the woman who looked more like a frail little grandmother than someone who had lied under oath and stolen the future for so many of the young men who left Henderson Ranch.

Paul Granger, although not as frail looking as his wife, came across as being innocent of conspiring with Theodore and accused the earlier witnesses of lying about what transpired after they left the Henderson Ranch. Like his wife before him, he painted a picture of someone who only wanted to help those he thought were inferior to himself and his wife.

Chris felt himself getting sick to his stomach. The only thing he'd ever been taught at the ranch that he felt was good was not to lie about anything.

"I can't take much more of this," he said, just loud enough for Cassion to hear.

In response, Cassion put his hand on Chris' knee. "Don't be too hasty. Granger is digging his own grave with every lie he tells. When I talked to the prosecutor, he assured me when the cross examination begins, he will be presenting the bank records for both Paul and Doreen Granger. I think you'll be surprised when you see what they reveal."

Before the cross examination could begin, the judge called a recess for the day. From the expression on Paul's face, Chris could tell he was relieved not to have to answer any more questions for the day. Perhaps the man was thinking he'd made a mistake in agreeing to take the stand in his own defense.

"They put on quite a show, didn't they?" Cassion asked as they left the courthouse. "Thank goodness, the jury didn't believe a word of what they said."

"How can you say that? They made it sound like we were the liars and they were clean as the freshly fallen snow."

"You concentrated too much on the lies they were telling. I, on the other hand, watched the faces of the jury. They were disgusted by every lie that came out of both of the defendant's mouths. It's evident they know what is truth and what is a lie. Tomorrow will be the turning point in this trial."

They went back to the hotel where they'd spent the previous night.

It was the same hotel where they'd stayed when they were at the same courthouse for the trial of the Hendersons. Even though Cassion insisted they needed to share the evening meal, all Chris wanted to do was go to his room and go to sleep.

"I can understand your need to be alone," Cassion said. "I'll make arrangements for your dinner to be sent to your room. You can't go without eating, because you'll need all your strength for the testimony that you'll be hearing tomorrow."

Chris thanked Cassion and made his way to the elevator that would take him to his room on the eleventh floor.

Once inside his room, he brought his communicator to life, to connect with Melian. Her face immediately filled the screen.

"Oh, Chris, I've been so worried about what was going on down there. Are you all right? You look so tired."

"I am tired. I did my best to answer every question honestly, only to hear the Grangers tell lie after lie even though they were under oath to tell the truth. It made me sick to my stomach when they called the other guys who testified against them, as well as me, bastards, ignorant and liars. I just want this to end. Cassion says tomorrow will be a different story, but I'm not as certain about that."

"You can trust Cassion. He knows what he's talking about."

Before they could continue their conversation, there was a knock at the door. When he went to answer it, a young man entered with a cart of food, followed by Cassion and Peter.

"I met Peter when he was going into the dining room. He was looking for you and I thought the two of you might enjoy sharing the evening meal. I will be eating with my contemporaries from Mexico. We all came here at the same time and rarely have an opportunity for face-to-face conversations."

Chris stepped aside so the food cart could be wheeled into the room. Once Cassion left, Chris ended his conversation with Melian and turned his attention to Peter.

Although Chris thought he wasn't hungry, the aroma coming from the food cart changed his mind.

"Are you as hungry as I am?" he asked Peter.

"I didn't think I was, but my mentor insisted I needed to eat. Now that I smell the food, I realize how hungry I actually am. I didn't eat much lunch. I guess it was because of nerves or it could be the fact I was used to not eating three meals a day when I worked on the ranch."

Chris nodded and started taking the covers from the dishes that contained their meal. Each plate was loaded with steaming roast beef, mashed potatoes drowning in rich beef gravy, and green beans. Other bowls on the cart contained a green salad with a light Italian dressing, as well as a piece of apple pie. Chilled bottles of water were also on the cart.

"It looks like a feast fit for a king," Chris observed.

From the look on Peter's face, Chris knew his friend had no idea of what a king was. He placed the food on the table along with the silverware.

It was amazing to see Peter wait until Chris started to eat before tentatively following his lead. It was rewarding to see the young man savoring each mouthful of food, as though it was the best food he'd ever eaten.

I know Peter is older than I am, but with the education I've been given and the manners I've been taught, I'm years beyond him.

"What was it like on the ranch?" he finally asked.

"Maybe I should start with leaving Henderson Ranch. Old man Henderson no more than left me off on the street of that town, than Pops approached me. He took me back to his house and got me some clean clothes. He suggested I put the hundred dollars Henderson gave me in the top dresser drawer for safe keeping."

Chris nodded. So far Peter's story mirrored his own right down to how he was told to put the money in the dresser drawer.

"That evening, Ma served us the evening meal. As I recall, she put the food on the plates before she gave it to us. I remember I could hardly able to keep my eyes open after we ate, so I went right to bed. The more I think about it, the more convinced I am that the food was drugged."

"Drugged?" Chris questioned. "I never thought about that, but I think you might be onto something. I remember going to bed almost as soon as we finished eating that night. You might be on to something, but of course, we could never prove it."

"I agree, but it's the only reason I think that's what happened. I've always been a light sleeper. That night I don't recall anything after I went to bed until Pops woke me up the next morning. That was when he said he'd found me work on a ranch in Mexico. He said the pay was good and since I knew a little Spanish I could do well working there. While I took a shower, Ma fixed us something to eat. I have to admit it was the best food I'd ever eaten until I was rescued and taken to the Alien complex."

"I felt the same way. I thought I'd never be hungry again until I got mixed up with Ernst and his group. The food was a little better than what we got at the ranch, but not by much."

Peter took another bit of his food before he began to speak again. "As soon as we finished eating, Pops and I got into his hovercraft and flew it down to the ranch in Mexico. As soon as we arrived, we were met by Senor Alfonso. He handed Pops some money and put an ankle bracelet on my right leg. He told me I was his, bought and paid for. From that moment on, my every move was monitored. For the first two weeks I was there, I was chained to my bed and indoctrinated into what was going to be expected of me on the ranch. I was to work from six in the morning until eight in the evening in the barns. There was only one meal a day and that was less than satisfactory. After a while, I was fitted for a collar and allowed to ride the range with the other slaves who worked there."

"When did you realize the money that Henderson gave you, was gone?" Chris asked.

"We were on the way to Mexico, I told Pops I'd forgotten to take it with me. He said he'd have Ma look for it and send it to me. Of course, no money ever arrived. I'm certain they took it."

"I'm afraid you're right. Cassion told me the prosecution is looking into their banking records. Do you remember when you were there with them?"

"It was about two months after you left. Time doesn't mean much to me, but I always counted the baths we got to take. Every time we took four baths, I knew another month had passed. It was eight baths between the time you left and the time I left."

Chris had forgotten about the fact baths were only available to them once a week. He thought swimming in the creek during the summer and being able to bathe with water heated on the stove twice weekly at Ernst's camp was luxury. Since coming to the complex he enjoyed his daily shower. How his priorities had changed over the past three years came as a marvelment to him.

"According to the information on my DNA chip, my birthday is in June, so that means you must have left in August."

They spent the remainder of the evening talking about their experiences since they were last together on Henderson Ranch.

It was getting late when Cassion returned to the suite. With him was Peter's alien mentor. "Have you two had enough time to get caught up?" Cassion asked.

"I doubt there will ever be enough time to learn everything Peter and the others have to tell me about their past," Chris replied. "Of course, we have a lifetime to get caught up. I'm certain our paths will be crossing many times in the future."

Once Peter and his mentor left the suite, Chris felt comfortable enough to tell Cassion everything he learned from his former friend.

"I tend to agree with you. The one hundred dollars was the payment from Henderson for the part the Granger's played in this scenario. What I don't understand is why Mr. Henderson would take Mark down to Mexico himself?"

"I wondered about that myself. From what Peter told me, Pops was given a great deal of money when he was left at Alfonso's ranch. I'll be anxious to see those banking records. I have a feeling Pops was sharing what he got when he released us to either the ranches in Mexico or to groups like Ernst's. It's possible that Henderson thought Mark was more valuable than most of them. Even without the translating chip, he was fluent in Spanish. He was also one of the best ranch hands, in spite of the bad treatment and less than nourishing food we got from the Hendersons."

"Why do you think he wanted to cut Pops out of the equation?"

Chris pondered his answer. At first, he wasn't sure what Cassion meant. From his classes he knew what the word equation meant.

"Even though there were still several kids at the ranch, they weren't arriving at the same rate as when I was younger. It's possible, splitting the money wasn't an option anymore. From what I can figure out, Peter was the last one of us released who went to Pops and Ma's home before being taken to their final destination."

"Would you be willing to be recalled to the stand to give additional testimony?"

Chris nodded his agreement. He had thought the Granger's to be his saviors, only to now realize they were part of the horrific events that were taking part on the Henderson Ranch.

Chapter Eighteen

Court was once again in session when the defense attorney rested his case. Immediately, the prosecutor asked to call a rebuttal witness to the stand.

Chris watched as Cassion took the stand and presented the financial statements he'd obtained for both Paul and Doreen Granger.

"What did you find in these statements?" the prosecuting attorney asked.

"Into the account for Doreen Granger, there were regular deposits of one hundred dollars. They all align perfectly with when each of the boys from the ranch was dropped off close to the Granger home. Days later, Paul Granger deposited large amounts of money into his account. Had we gotten financial records for Theodor Henderson, I'm certain we would have seen similar deposits on corresponding dates to those made by Mr. Granger. These deposits into the Granger account were no longer made after Peter was taken to Mexico. We know, for certain, there were other young men who aged out of the program at the ranch after Peter did, but by that time there were no more deposits into the Granger's accounts. It is our assumption that the Hendersons needed additional finances."

Chris listened intently to what Cassion was testifying to. He knew he was going to be called back to the stand. Earlier when he'd testified, he faced the Grangers as he remembered them. This time, he would have to face the same people, only they looked more like very elderly and sick people who didn't deserve what was happening to them.

When he was called to the stand, they both glared at him with contempt. They were no longer the saviors he once thought them to be. With all the information he'd been given in the last few hours, he saw them more like the predators they were.

"You are still under oath," the prosecutor informed him.

Chris nodded.

"You indicated that the Grangers were good to you. Why then did you want to take the stand again?"

"My friend, Peter, and I had a long talk last night. We were each given a hundred dollars from Mr. Henderson. He told us that we were to use the money to start our new lives. Everything happened so quickly while I was with them, I didn't think about the money again until I was with Patrick's group. When I mentioned it, Patrick told me that since I was with him, I didn't need it and to forget about it."

"How long were you at the Granger home before you went with Patrick Ernst?"

"It was interesting. As soon as I mentioned I'd been told about Patrick Ernst, Pops was able to contact him. It was as though he was waiting for me to mention Ernst's name. I left three days after I arrived."

The prosecutor returned to his seat and the defense attorney got to his feet. "Are you certain you were given money when you left the Henderson ranch?"

The question caught Chris off guard. "How could I forget something like that? In all my life, I'd never had money. I had no idea of what it was for or how to use it. I was in awe of holding something like that in my hands."

"Are you certain you didn't take the money with you and are making all of this up to make Mr. and Mrs. Granger look guilty?"

Chris was appalled by the accusation. "I was abused as a child and more so when I became an adult. It wasn't the physical abuse I suffered at the hands of Mr. and Mrs. Henderson. The abuse I suffered while with Patrick Ernst was mental and emotional. Nevertheless, the one thing I was taught as a child and a young adult the most important thing in life was to tell the truth, no matter what the consequences. I didn't want to believe that the Grangers were part of the abuse going on at Henderson Ranch, but from everything I've learned, they are not as innocent as they want everyone to believe."

There were no more questions and with relief, Chris left the stand and returned to his seat next to Cassion.

Closing arguments were made and the jury was sent back to the jury room for deliberations. For Chris, the morning had been draining. More than anything else, he wanted to return to the suite and take a nap, but Cassion assured Chris he needed to eat as he'd hardly touched his breakfast.

Food held little appeal, but he obliged Cassion by ordering a bowl of soup along with a salad. He ate enough to pacify Cassion, when someone came from the court to tell them that the jury had returned with their verdict.

"I can't believe how quickly they came to their decision," Cassion said, as they made their way back to the courthouse.

"Is that good or bad?"

"It's hard to tell. Hopefully they saw through the façade the defense tried to show. Only time will tell."

Once inside the courthouse, Chris was surprised to see the Grangers enter the room. Although they looked frail hours earlier, now they looked as though they were on death's door.

Everyone took their seats and the jury handed their decision to the judge. After looking at the paper she turned her attention to the jury. "Is this your unanimous decision?"

The foreperson of the jury stood and affirmed their decision had been unanimous.

The judge instructed the Grangers to stand to hear the verdict.

"Paul and Doreen Granger, you have been found guilty of all of the charges leveled against you. At this time this court is sentencing you to life imprisonment in the penal colony under the ice cap of the Antarctica. Following these proceedings, you will be taken directly there to begin your sentence."

Chris watched as Doreen collapsed and Paul tried to keep her from falling to the floor. As if the effort was too much for him, he relied on their attorney to help him support his wife's weight.

After Doreen was revived, Paul turned toward the people assembled to watch the proceedings. "This is your fault," he said, pointing directly at both Chris and Peter. "You'll rot in hell for what you've done to us."

Chris wanted to reply, but Cassion stopped him. "Don't stoop to his level," Cassion whispered. "He's not worth it."

Chris nodded. Without saying a word, he watched as Paul and Doreen were led out of the courtroom by two aliens wearing the uniforms of guards from the penal colony.

"It's over," Chris said.

"For you, yes, but I still have to testify at the trial for Senor Alfonso. I wish you well, my friend. Again, thank you for saving me as well as many others from the horrors we've lived through for most of our lives. I pray we will meet again in the future."

~ * ~

Melian waited for Chris at the complex. As soon as he came into the facility, she was ready to have him enfold her in his arms.

"I missed you so much," she said, as she wound her arms around his neck. "I watched the proceedings on my communicator. It had to be terrible for you. Are you certain they will never be able to hurt anyone again?"

"Positive. They were taken directly to the penal colony under the ice cap of the Antarctica. Do you know anything about that place?"

A look of horror crossed Melian's face. "My grandfather was the first warden of that place. It is where the worst of the worst criminals are taken. As frail as the Grangers looked in the courtroom, it is doubtful they will live more than a few months."

"Don't let their appearance in court fool you. At the beginning of the trial, you would have seen a completely different couple. Their frail appearance was little more than an act to win the sympathy of the jury. It will not be their health that will determine how long they will survive. Their crimes were not as terrible as those of the Hendersons, but they still took advantage of young men who had no idea of what was being done to them. Worse yet they profited from it. Although the accounts show that Ma took the money given to us by Mr. Henderson, Pops shared the money that was paid for the delivery of the young men they took advantage of. They are both guilty."

Any sympathy Melian had for the Grangers seemed to dissipate as the reality of the situation began to set in.

"How can people be so cruel? I've been studying the history Caroline has been writing down. In it she told of how slavery tore this country apart in the nineteenth century. I had no idea anything like it would still be going on in modern times. It's such an atrocity. I thank the One God that you were able to get away from that situation and found your way here. I know you have a bright future ahead of you."

Chris knew the words he wanted to say to Melian, but he was afraid to say them. He read about love. He saw it between Caroline and Aaron as well as the members of his family. He thought about the word family. It was something unknown to him. He knew before he could proclaim his love for Melian, he would have to come to grips with his feelings and learn the true meaning of love.

~ * ~

The following Monday, it seemed as though the trial had never happened. Chris made his way to class and Mark joined him.

"I watched the trial," Mark greeted him.

"It sounds like everyone did. That was quite a show the Grangers put on."

"It certainly was. I never knew them but the difference between when they first came into the courtroom and when they returned for the afternoon session was dramatic. In a way, I wish Henderson would have dropped me off in town. It sounds like for the one night you were with the Grangers, you were treated well."

"I was, but when I learned their part in what happened to those of us who crossed their path it makes me sick to my stomach. I was lucky that Henderson wanted me sent to Patrick's group. At least it wasn't slave labor, but the conditions weren't much better."

Their conversation ended when Hodia entered the classroom to begin their morning's lesson. Although Chris expected to enjoy a math class, he was surprised when the subject of this morning's class was Civics and the workings of the legal system. Since both Chris and Mark had recently been in the courtroom for trials, Hodia explained they needed to know more about how things worked.

"In both of your cases, they were dealing with very serious crimes. It is extremely unusual for Earthlings to be sent to either the penal colony on the dark side of the moon or under the ice cap of the Antarctica. Both of these are maximum security facilities. Life there will not be easy for either the Hendersons on the dark side of the moon or for the Grangers under the ice cap of the Antarctica."

Chris raised his hand. "I feel the punishment fits the crime for the Hendersons, but wasn't it a bit severe for the Grangers?"

"I don't think so," Hodia replied. "They didn't participate for the first eighteen years of your lives, but they profited from selling many young adults to either the ranches in Mexico or to groups with the same ideals as Patrick Ernst. You have to know; we have been looking into not only the ranches but also the militant groups. There are more arrests and trials that will be coming in the future. Slavery, no matter what form it takes, was outlawed in the United States, over two hundred years ago."

Chris thought of the lessons Caroline taught, and although he knew that the slavery of the seventeenth and eighteenth century seemed to be a thing of the past, he knew what he'd endured was relatively close to that situation.

As much as he wanted all of this to be behind him, he knew the end would not be in sight for many months or maybe years in the future.

--

Chapter Nineteen

With the trials Chris had to participate in finally over, he pledged his loyalty to Mark as he struggled with the upcoming trial for the owner of the ranch in Mexico where he had been worked almost to death.

At long last the trial began. Chris was surprised at the numbers of cowboys who came to testify alongside of Mark.

Through this trial, Chris learned the involvement of the Hendersons and the Grangers was only the tip of the iceberg. There were many other facilities throughout North and South America who had supplied young men to these ranches. Now that they were being tried, for human trafficking and slavery, he realized this would mean there would be a big influx of young men in need of education and jobs.

As had been the situation during the other trials, Mark and Chris shared a suite at a local hotel with Cassion. With the proceedings completed for the day, the three of them ordered room service to discuss the ramifications of the information that had been disclosed during the proceedings.

"Are you thinking what I'm thinking?" Mark asked.

Chris thought for a moment before answering. "I think so. I know that we've been planning to turn Henderson Ranch into a home for unwanted children, but after today, I see the need is for those of us who have aged out of the system and have no education or any training for employment other than ranching."

"I see what you're getting at," Cassion agreed. "With George's people financing the ranch, I think my people could easily build a complex on the land and use it for the reeducation of these young men. You've come so far in your studies, Chris, it is possible with Melian's help you can become the administrator of this facility. Of course, Hodia and myself would be willing to relocate there to help in any capacity you need us."

Mark smiled broadly. "I believe the two of you have read my mind. Listening to the men who testified today, I see that I'm not alone. You've given me a great chance. I may not be as smart as my friend Chris, but I do understand that the men we met today need the same chance. I realize we were all trained to be ranch hands, but there are other things we can do. While Chris' path seems to be mathematical as well as leadership, my path seems to be taking a different direction. I love the ranch work. That said, Kara has opened my eyes to a new direction in my life. I'd like to study to become a veterinarian. I've already started working on courses as well as working with some of the top vets at the complex. I have a long way to go, but if we turn the ranch into an educational mecca, I think some of the people I've met in Denver will be willing to come with us and start this new adventure with us."

Chris was shocked at what Mark was saying. He'd been so absorbed in his own training and ambitions; he hadn't kept up with what his friend was doing with the opportunity he'd been given.

"Do you think we can pull this off, Cassion?" Chris asked.

"It will take time to set everything up, but the two of you need more time for your schooling. Maybe we can get this opened by the end of the year. It would mean that the two of you would have to continue your education once we're up and running. Do you think you would be able to agree to that?"

"I would," Chris replied. "Before I make the move, I'd like to ask Melian to be my wife. Do you know how I can contact her parents for permission to marry her?"

Cassion smiled. "I've anticipated this happening. When Melian came to Denver with her aunt, Zora, her father asked if I would become her legal guardian. She is young and I can understand his concern of sending her so far from her home. Her father and I have been in contact and we both are agreeable with such a mating. Rather than our permission, I suggest you ask her for yourself."

Chris felt a rush of relief as he listened to what Cassion was telling him.

"I have the same question to ask about Kara. The two of us have become very close since I came to the complex. I would like to have her as my wife."

"Kara is the daughter of Dr. Aragon. I doubt there will be any objection to the two of you becoming man and wife. Once you speak to Dr. Aragon, I suggest you ask Kara about her feelings. If they are the same as yours, there is no reason you shouldn't go into this new venture together."

~ * ~

A week after the first trial of the ranchers who participated in the slave labor, Chris and Mark returned to the complex in Denver.

As it had been in the past, Melian was at the spaceport to meet Chris and say how much she'd missed him.

That evening, over dinner, Chris broached the question he'd been rehearsing ever since the conversation he'd had with Mark and Cassion days earlier.

"I have a question to ask of you," he began.

Melian put her finger to his lips. "I think I know what you want to ask me. My father contacted me to say Cassion had told him of what he thought was going on between the two of us. Cassion also contacted me to tell me about the plans you have for the new complex at Henderson Ranch. I am so excited about all the plans that are being made. I know we're both young, but…"

"Did anyone ever tell you; you talk too much? I want to ask you to become my wife and partner in life."

Even before giving her verbal answer, Melian's eyes sparkled with excitement. "I would be pleased to become your wife."

With her acceptance, Chris realized he had no ring to give her. "I have a feeling I might have jumped the gun a bit. I have nothing to give you as a symbol of my love for you."

"I don't need a fancy ring. That will come in time. For now, it's enough to know we have a wonderful life stretching before us. I can hardly wait to tell our families of our great news."

Chris thought about telling his family. Would they be happy for him or would they think he was jumping into something too quickly?

The first communication they made was to Melian's family at their stronghold under the ice cap of the Antarctica.

Her mother cried and her father congratulated Chris on his choice for his partner for life. They both said they were planning a trip to the Denver complex in order to be part of the arrangements for their upcoming wedding.

Chris was more apprehensive about contacting his family with the news they had to share. He decided it would be best if he contacted his mother's side of the family first.

George wanted to plan a Native American service on the reservation. He said it was only right because his mother had been cheated out of the traditional service that she deserved.

When he placed the call to Illinois, he found his grandmother was the most excited about his announcement.

"Have you picked out a ring yet?" Felica inquired.

"Not yet, Grandma. Why do you ask?"

"I know it might be a bit old fashioned, but I have the ring that was given to my mother when she became engaged to my father. It was meant to go to your father so he could give it to your mother. Let me get it. If you think it is something that Melian would enjoy wearing, I will send it to you."

Together they waited while Felicia retrieved the ring that she'd been keeping it all these years.

"What do you think?" Chris asked Melian as they waited.

"I think it's the most romantic thing I've ever heard of. When I was a little girl, I read a lot of the romance novels my parents bought for me from the stores on Earth. That was a romantic gesture that I always thought was old fashioned. Now I think it's absolutely lovely."

Felicia's image filled the screen as she opened up a beautiful purple velvet jewelry box. Inside, nestled in a deeper shade of purple, was a beautiful diamond ring in a solid gold setting. With it was a matching wedding band and a second box that housed a man's wedding band that was the perfect match to the first set.

"I know it's old fashioned, but do you children think these are something you might enjoy having as your commitment rings?"

"Oh, they're beautiful," Melian declared. "I don't think they're at all old fashioned. They are part of Chris' family. I would be honored to wear them."

"It sounds like that's settled," Chester said. "I've been looking into a few things for you, myself. I've found an account that our father set up for your father. It's been drawing interest for years. Last week, I put your name on the account. You are not without finances. That, added to the work I've been doing with the tribal council, gives me a feeling your future, as well as Mark's, is going to be quite secure. George called me after he talked to Cassion and we're all excited about the plans you and Mark are making for the ranch."

"I-I didn't know things had progressed that far," Chris stammered.

"You'll get used to it. Since we spent time with your family on the reservation, George and I have become good friends. We're both very driven business men. The plans Cassion shared with George are very intriguing. They're much more exciting than a school for children who might no longer need your help in the future. The way it sounds, you and Melian will be able to work with young men and teach then the things they need to know. The aliens have pledged their assistance, and I have partners who are excited by this project as well."

"How soon are the two of you planning your wedding?" Susan said, her image replacing that of her brother on the screen.

"We don't know," Melian said. "This is all very new to us. My parents are planning to come to help with the wedding planning, Chris' Uncle George wants us to have a Native American ceremony. We need time to figure this all out."

"Of course, you do, my dear," Felicia added. "I will have a courier pick up the rings this afternoon. When you are ready to make wedding plans, I would be honored to come out to Denver, meet your parents and help with the preparations. Right now, I am certain you are overwhelmed by all of this."

They continued talking for a few minutes before ending the conversation.

"I think this will be one interesting wedding," Chris said, pulling Melian into his embrace. "Do your parents have any traditions I should know about?"

"A few. How would you feel about having three ceremonies?"

"Three? Are you sure?"

"Positive. The wedding traditions of my people are very different from those of our friends here on Earth. I am certain the ceremony George is talking about is very different as well. We are melding three heritages. It is only fitting that we honor all of those heritages. I think this will be an interesting wedding, to say the very least."

Chapter Twenty

Chris returned to his classes, but his mind drifted between the plans for Henderson Ranch as well as his wedding to Melian.

"I have a feeling history is not what is on your mind today," Caroline said.

"I'm sorry, there are just so many things going on right now, I'm having trouble concentrating."

"I honestly don't blame you. Aaron and I have been looking over your plans for Henderson Ranch and we want to be involved. I have learned I love teaching history. Besides it will be a heathy place for Jonathan to grow up. Do you think you and Mark would be willing to allow us to come there to help you?"

The fact his teacher was asking for his permission to join him in Nevada came as a shock. "I don't know if I'm the person who should be making that decision."

"Nonsense, who better to make the decision. This project has come about because of what happened to you and Mark. The two of you are the ones who came up with this the idea, your family, both sides, are behind you on this project, in other words, this is your idea and therefore you're considered the administrator of the new Henderson Ranch."

"If that's so, I don't think the name Henderson Ranch is appropriate."

"What do you suggest?"

"I've been thinking about that. What do you think of Resurrection Ranch? The brand could be RR. I know Mark wants to run cattle as a cash crop and he also wants to become a vet. I could see a top veterinarian school there, along with other schools Cassion and I have been talking about."

"That certainly sounds interesting. Do you have any idea how many young men will be there?"

"So far, we have located about ten others who would be interested, that does include Peter. I knew him from the ranch and he was one of the people who testified against the Grangers at their trial. We got reacquainted during that time. He knows of three others from the ranch he was working at in Mexico who would be willing to be educated and relocated. Cassion says he's been contacted by four others who were also working on ranches that were raided. That makes ten counting Mark and me. There are three we haven't accounted for as of yet and three younger children who haven't found their family. That makes ten with Peter. Add Mark and me to the group and that makes our number twelve. I understand the two of us still need more education than we've received since we arrived here."

"This is so exciting, when do you think you will be able to make the move?"

"With summer and the end of classes for three months, we are hoping to go out there for the summer. Most of us are good at carpentry, and we should be able to update the main house as well as the dormitory. We also are thinking of building an apartment complex for any of us who are married as well as the teachers who have pledged to join us."

"It sounds like you have many plans. Will you be getting any help from your family?"

"I've already contacted both sides of my family. There are volunteers from the reservation who have gone down to the ranch to oversee the ranching aspect and to begin the building projects. People who work for Uncle Chester in Chicago are also going to be arriving soon with not only people who are willing to do physical labor, but also financial assistance. Things are moving so quickly it's hard to keep up with everything."

Caroline smiled at him as a sign of her reassurance he was doing the right thing with his life.

"What about Melian? Will she be going with you?"

"That's something else. We are planning to be married before we move to Nevada. It's going to be quite interesting, since Melian's family wants a ceremony in the traditions of her people. The Native American side of my family wants us to be married in their tradition, and of course, the white side of my family wants a Christian ceremony. I have a feeling there will be three ceremonies before all is said and done. I do hope you and Aaron will be able to be with us through it all."

"We wouldn't miss it for anything in the world."

Knowing the lesson for the day wouldn't be finished, they both went to their apartments for the remainder of the afternoon.

~ * ~

By the end of the week, the complex buzzed with activity. The Jennings family arrived to make preparations with the pastor of the church for the Christian ceremony. Melian's family arrived with a priest from their community to confer with the pastor as well as the Jennings family in making arrangements to meld the two services condoned by the One God into one.

Last to arrive were Chris' mother's side of the family. This was the one fraction of the three families that worried Chris the most. How would their plans for a Native American ceremony coincide with the plans that were being made for a ceremony at the church?

~ * ~

The morning of the wedding dawned bright. The sunshine of late May accented the newly budded green leaves of the trees and the beauty of the garden.

Inside the church, the combined service featuring the pastor of the complex church and the priest who came from under Antarctica's ice cap, followed their traditions and prepared for the service to unite Chris and Melian.

Chris paced the small room behind the altar nervously. This was a big step in his life and with little experience of a loving relationship he prayed to the One God he would be able to make Melian happy for the remainder of their lives.

"I am certain Melian is as nervous as you are," Chester advised him.

"I tend to agree," George chimed in. "Since we are almost ready for the ceremony to begin, I suggest we go out to the sanctuary and join our wives. Soon you will be saying the vows that will seal your future with Melian."

Chris pondered the words of the uncles from both sides of his family. He was embarking on yet another unknown adventure in his life and he prayed he would be the best husband Melian could have ever imagined.

"I know what this ceremony is going to be, because both Melian and I have been counseled by the pastor as well as the priest. What we don't know is what the Native American ceremony will entail."

"That, my boy, will be a pleasant surprise. After the formal ceremony is performed, we will adjourn to the garden, where the last ceremony will take place. Rather than religious, it is symbolic of the journey you and Melian are embarking upon."

Without saying more, Chester and George left Chris and Mark to wait for their cue to enter the sanctuary.

It didn't take long for both the pastor and the priest to come into the room and escort Chris and Mark to their places at the front of the church.

In front of them, Chris saw a mixed congregation. There before them were members of both sides of Chris' family and young men who had been rescued because of what Chris told the authorities about the atrocities happing at Henderson Ranch. They sat interspersed with Aliens from the complex, the dark side of the moon, and under Antarctica's ice cap. Not only was it an explementary coming together of several cultures, it was a bonding between the races.

Kara was the first to make the walk down the center aisle of the church. The deep purple of her gown accented her coloring and her violet eyes perfectly. She carried a bouquet of deep purple, lavender and white carnations.

Chris smiled when Mark stepped forward to take her arm and led her to stand to the left of where Melian would soon stand as they pledged their lives to each other for all time.

After Kara took her place, Melian and her father entered the church. If Chris had not met him before, he would have found the man to be quite intimidating. He stood almost seven feet tall, was very muscular and his piercing gaze came from eyes a deeper shade of violet than Melian's.

Melian's gown was made from a beautiful purple satin with an overskirt and bodice of white lace. The lace sleeves were sheer and accented her long arms beautifully. Beneath the full skirt, he was certain were several petticoats, as Melian called them, to make the skirt float around her with each step. In her hand she held a bouquet of the same colors as those Kara carried, but these were roses, specially grown and imported for the wedding. Her beauty took his breath away and he wondered how he had been lucky enough to have won her love.

When it came time for the vows to be said, Chris repeated, word for word, what the pastor told him. It was the same with the vows Melian said. For her, it was the priest who first said the words that would seal their lives as one for eternity.

Time seemed to fly and almost as soon as the ceremony began Chris was kissing his wife for the first time as a married couple.

After greeting their guests, they went out to the garden where the reception was being held. Chris was amazed to see the shaman who came with the Native American side of his family, dressed in traditional regalia. A beautiful arch had been built from a white wickerlike material and the shaman stood under it. On each side of the arch was a pile of sticks that blazed beautifully. In the center was a larger pile of wood.

Once they stood in front of the arch, the shaman began to make his speech.

"Today, our brother, Christopher, and our sister, Melian, are joining their lives together for all eternity. To the north, the fire is representative of the life that Christopher has lived and to the south the fire represents Melian's life. Please, step forward, and with these sticks, push both fires into the center. Your past lives are in the past and the new lives you are embarking upon will become the center of your future. So shall your life fires be joined into one that no one, other than the Great Spirit, the One God, can ever separate."

Chris smiled as he pushed his small fire into the larger stack of wood. At the same time, Melian beamed while she moved her fire to join his. He was glad he had no idea of the service that would join them as one in the Native American tradition. It was a beautiful end to a perfect day. Their joining in three entirely different ceremonies, was something that would not soon be forgotten.

Alone in a New World
The New World Book Three

As a child of four, Marco is all alone in the world. With only his mother in his life, her death prompts the authorities to send him to Henderson Ranch for boys. At the age of eighteen, he is sold into slavery to a ranch in Mexico. Two years later, he is recued and reunited with his childhood friend, Christopher. At his friend's insistence he modernizes his name to Mark and embarks on a journey that will bring him full circle back to Henderson Ranch, now called Resurrection Ranch. On his journey, Mark finds previously unknown family and love with one of the alien nurses, Kara, all off whom are willing to journey with him into the future at Resurrection Ranch.

Chapter One
October, 2104

Jason Culver was on the late-night patrol in Elko, Nevada. He checked the communicator on his wrist and saw the time was four thirty in the morning. His shift would be ending in two and a half hours. This was going to be his last late shift. Beginning tomorrow, he would be transferring to the day shift of the Elko Police Department. He was more than ready to get on a regular day schedule like most of the other people in the world. What he did realize was this had been a good shift for him, at least when he was single. Most people were at home in bed and not out doing mischief or breaking laws. On the day shift he would see much more action.

His mental musings were interrupted when he saw something in his headlights that caused him to land his hover craft and go to investigate what seemed to be too bazar to be true.

Once he left his craft, he hurried to where a little boy, wearing pajamas with no shoes, stood on the sidewalk crying.

"I'm officer Culver," he said as he approached the child. "Where is your mother?"

The boy sniffed loudly and proclaimed in heavily accented English, "My mama won't wake up."

Jason knelt in front of the child. "What's your name?"

"Marco."

"Do you know where you live?"

He nodded his head and pointed to an apartment complex.

"Did you have a bad dream?"

Marco shook his head.

"It's very late. This is the time when everyone should be in bed sleeping. Let me take you to your apartment. I'm certain your mother is very worried about you."

Again, Marco shook his head. "She's been asleep for a long time. I tried to wake her up when I got up when it was daytime. She wouldn't wake up. I'm hungry."

Jason noticed the child's words, although they were spoken in English, sometimes sounded more like Spanish. Looking closer, he could tell the boy was of Mexican descent. It was possible his mother was in the country illegally. There could be drugs involved. Anything was possible.

Picking Marco up, he made his way inside the building. After checking the listing of tenants, he saw the name Tessa Almanor. It was the only name that sounded as though it could be Mexican. The apartment number beside the name was two fifty-two.

Rather than taking the elevator, Jason carried Marco up the stairs to the second floor. The door with the right number stood open. Before entering, Jason put the child down.

"I'm going to check on your mother. You stay here."

His heart pounded almost out of his chest as he made his way through the dark apartment. He shown his flashlight around the neat living room as well as the pristine kitchen. It looked like Tessa kept a clean house. To his right, was a hallway. It led down to a bathroom and two doors what looked like they led into bedrooms. In the first room, he saw a single bed, with decorations that denoted it belonged to a small child. Moving on, he went into the room where he could see a woman sleeping on the bed.

"Ms. Almanor? Can you hear me?"

When he received no response, he touched her shoulder. To his horror, her skin was cold and her body stiff. It was evident she'd been dead for several hours.

He immediately contacted his superior officer on his communicator. He also requested the medical examiner as well as social services and back-up.

Remembering Marco, he hurried back out into the hall. The child was still whimpering, although now his cries weren't loud, big tears rolled down his cheeks as he sucked his thumb.

"Do you know where your father is?" Jason asked.

Without taking his thumb from his mouth, Marco shook his head no.

"Do you have other family here in town?"

Again, the child indicated no.

It wasn't long before social services arrived and took the child away. With his duty to little Marco finished, he returned to the apartment. He started going through the rooms, looking for any information that would help him find the family of either the deceased woman or the child. He was shocked to see there were no papers identifying either Tessa or Marco. It was entirely possible those weren't even their names.

"What do we have here?" his superior officer asked when he entered the apartment with the medical examiner.

"I saw a little boy out on the sidewalk at four thirty this morning. He was wearing pajamas with no shoes and he was crying. He said his mother wouldn't wake up. I was certain he'd had a bad dream and woke up frightened. I brought him into this building and surmised the apartment rented under the name of Tessa Almanor had to belong to his mother. I left him in the hall and found his mother in the bedroom. It's evident she's been dead for several hours."

"Do you suspect foul play?"

Jason thought for a moment "I don't think so. The apartment is too neat to have a murder take place here. There also wasn't any blood that I could see. It's possible she died of natural causes."

"Where is the boy now?"

"Social services got here before you did. They took him. He was very distraught and he said he was hungry. He's only three, maybe four and just thinks his mother is sleeping. From what I gathered, he tried to wake her up yesterday when he got up and he couldn't. He's probably been alone ever since. It's possible he went out onto the street to see if someone could wake up his mother."

"Well, if that don't beat all. We've got to find out where the kid's father or any other relatives are. If we don't…"

Before his supervisor could continue, the medical examiner came out of the bedroom. "I won't know anything until we do an autopsy, but it looks like she might have suffered either a massive heart attack or an aneurism. What have you found out about her identity?"

"Next to nothing," Jason replied. "We'll know more when we can talk to the owner of this apartment building in the morning. He can probably shed some light on her background."

~ * ~

The woman who took Marco's hand and led him away from the apartment he'd shared with his mother, seemed nice enough. She tried to ask him several questions, but he remembered what his mother told him about talking to strangers.

We can't let him find us, Marco. If he does, he'll take you away from me and I'll never see you again.

His mother's words of warning rang in his head. Remembering them, he could hear the bad man who wanted Marco to call him Papa. They ran away from him and left their home in Arizona in the middle of the night. He also remembered his mother calling him Paco but telling him from now on he would be called Marco.

Even though the nice lady got him some food to eat, he knew he had to protect the secret his mother told him never to tell.

~ * ~

Two weeks into the investigation, Jason knew no more about Tessa Almanor than he had the morning he found her dead in her bed.

He didn't know how many times he'd read the report from the medica examiner. What it showed was that in the past she'd suffered a severe beating, so severe that it had cause her a slow and painful death from the internal bruising.

The interview with the owner of the apartment building didn't give them any more information that they already had. Tessa and her son moved into the furnished apartment less than two weeks before her death and she'd paid him cash for the first two month's rent. Other than that, he had no further information. Knowing the area where the apartment building was located, he realized cash talked very loudly and often it paid for no questions asked about someone's past.

To add insult to injury, he'd heard from social services, that since no family could be found for Marco, he'd been sent to a boy's ranch in a remote area of Nevada called Henderson Ranch. It was probably the best thing that could have happened to the boy. He would be able to grow up in a healthy environment. Being an orphan, as well as his Mexican heritage, made his chances of being adopted slim to none.

Awake in a New World
The New World Book One

Caroline Lewis feels life isn't worth living when she loses her husband to Covid-19 while on a business trip to China. In order to avoid the coming pandemic, she opts to have her body frozen to be awakened in 2070. In 2120, archaeologists exploring the ruins of Los Angeles, find Caroline's perfectly preserved body. As she is brought to life, fifty years later than expected, she is forced to learn to live in a world unlike the one she remembers from 2020. Aaron Phillips knows Caroline is special when he hires her as a research volunteer at the library. He hopes she feels the same way about.

Prologue

"I'm scared to death about this virus. From what my husband said, he suffered greatly before his death. I've had a premonition about this spreading not only to the U.S. but to the entire world," Caroline said. "Do you really think you can help me?"

The technician at the Cryogenics Lab examined the paperwork Caroline filled out earlier. "It looks like you're a good candidate for our services, Ms. Lewis. So far you have no symptoms of the virus, making you an ideal choice. You do know our services don't come for free."

Caroline reached into her purse and pulled out a stack of hundred-dollar bills. "From what I've read, you charge twenty thousand dollars. I have that amount right here. If you think you're going to raise the price just because of this virus, I'll leave right now."

"Don't be hasty, Ms. Lewis. Although there has been talk about raising the price, because of the current situation, no one has acted upon it. The twenty thousand will completely cover it. We can set your appointment for four thirty tomorrow afternoon. How long do you want to be frozen for?"

Caroline thought for a moment. With the virus spreading throughout the world, she prayed a cure would be found within the next fifty years. "I think until March of 2070 should be sufficient time. I'll see you tomorrow."

She left the office, secure in the knowledge that by this time tomorrow, she would be freeze dried until this pandemic was eradicated once and for all.

~ * ~

"Are you out of your mind, Caroline?" her brother Jonathan asked when she arrived at his home for supper that evening. "How could you throw away twenty thousand dollars on something this foolish? Those guys are nothing but shysters. Who knows what will happen to you in that place? I'm not ready to lose my sister."

"I'm willing to take that chance. My premonition about this virus, combined with my compromised immune system, is almost a death sentence in and of itself. If I can wake up fifty years in the future and not have to worry about any of these health problems, it's worth a shot. You know my husband was in China when this thing broke out and he died there. Other than you, I have no one else I care about left. This is the ideal solution for me."

"It's your decision and your money. Who am I to stop you, other than being your baby brother? I wish you well and I hope the future you're looking forward to is everything you want it to be."

"The cost of what I'm planning to do is only minimal considering what I'm worth. I have a document I want you to sign. It will transfer all of my assets to you. All I ask is that you take a minute part of them and invest wisely, so I will have money to live on when they awaken me in fifty years. I promise, I will come back to you. You are much younger than me and I am certain you will still be alive in 2070. We will meet again."

Chapter One

Los Angeles 2120

"I don't know what you're looking to find here, Nick. Los Angeles has been a wasteland since the pandemic, combined with the forces of nature, destroyed everything and everyone on the west coast a hundred years ago."

"It has, Lori, but something tells me we will make a find of great importance here. It could set the archaeology community on its ear with the biggest discovery of this century. We've got another three hours of time before they're expecting us back at headquarters. Let's just take a look through the ruins of this building."

Lori looked at the sign above the ruined building in front of them. "Cryogenics? What do you think that means?"

Nick stopped in his tracks, pulling up the Internet on his watch. After typing in the word that seemed alien to both of them, he waited for the response. "Let's see, it says that during the late twentieth and early twenty-first century, cryogenics was the freezing of human bodies to be awakened in the future when there was hope there would be a cure for some of the diseases plaguing the planet at that time. From what it says here, the quacks that promised eternal life through freezing the body in liquid nitrogen made a bundle off the people who came to them. It says here that people paid ten thousand dollars in the beginning and it went to twenty thousand dollars after the turn of the century. By the time the pandemic was at its peak, the price skyrocketed to over fifty thousand dollars. The people who were promoting this crap became millionaires overnight, for all the good it did them."

Lori thought about this history she'd learned, not only in high school but in college. The pandemic of 2020 had encompassed the world within a matter of weeks and disappeared just as quickly. With the world in chaos, it was the ideal time for World War III to be launched. Before it could, natural disasters wreaked havoc on both the east and west coasts of the United States, leaving millions of their citizens dead or dying. Now, a hundred years later, the government had declared the areas safe for the archeological teams to come in to reap the benefits of the knowledge from one hundred years ago in the hopes of keeping something like this from happening again.

"Okay, it won't hurt to go in there," Lori conceded. "It could prove quite interesting."

Carefully, they picked their way through the ruins of what once must have been a beautiful building. The lobby still sported a spectacular marble floor with the remains of what once must have been a receptionist desk. In front of them a spiral staircase led to a now non-existent second floor. To the right of it were stairs leading to what must have been a basement.

With trepidation, they made their way down the steps. Without the sunlight that illuminated the upper floor, they each switched on their flashlights as well as the lamps on their hardhats. As they did, they saw several chambers, with decaying bodies of men and women inside of the glass protective doors that looked like they cracked sometime over the past century, allowing the nitrogen gas to leak out and destroy them.

"So much for preserving eternal life," Lori quipped. "All they got for their tens of thousands of dollars was just as dead as anyone else. What a scam."

"Maybe not. Look here, this one is really well preserved. We'd better radio the team and see if anyone knows how to reverse this process. Think of the possibilities if we could resurrect a woman from 2020 or maybe before."

"I think you're right about 2020. There's a tag on the outside of her chamber and it says her name is Caroline Lewis and she was frozen on March 17, 2020."

It didn't take long for Nick to hurry up the stairs in order to make contact with their base camp. While he did, Lori continued to look at not only the decaying bodies, but the perfectly preserved body of the woman named Caroline drew her like a magnet.

"Why did you do it, Caroline?" she asked aloud, knowing she wouldn't get an answer.

As she continued to look around, she found a cabinet with several three ring binders in it. Being careful with the binders, she finally found one with the name of Caroline Lewis printed on the spine of the book.

She'd just pulled it out when Nick reappeared.

"I got a hold of Dr. Jamison and she is researching how to handle this. She said she should be here within the hour. Our instructions are to stay and guard this find until she gets here. I have a feeling this discovery is going to make us as famous as the archaeologists who discovered King Tut's tomb back in the early twentieth century."

"If I remember my history correctly, they all fell victim to a curse the ancient Egyptian put on Tut's tomb. I hope there isn't any kind of curse out on Caroline."

"Now you're being paranoid. Curses were things from ancient history and the dark ages. People were too advanced in the twenty-first century to believe in those things."

Lori agreed with Nick. There were no such things as curses but the three-ring binders she'd found in the file drawer could shed some light on the people in the damaged cryogenics chambers.

"I found these binders. The only one I took out was the one with Caroline's name on it. Since we have to wait for Dr. Jamison, we might as well see what it says about our sleeping beauty."

Lori opened the book and smiled to see the pages were encased in protective plastic. At least they wouldn't be too fragile to be touched.

"Caroline Lewis, female, forty-two years of age, no sign of the virus. Even though she suffered from breast cancer in 2017, she is cancer free," she read aloud. "It also says she paid twenty thousand dollars to the facility for her chance at eternal life. She wanted to be reawakened in 2070. Oh well, Caroline, you're only about fifty years overdue. I wonder how you will react to the state the world is in today."

Nick nodded his agreement. "We should take the remainder of the binders back to headquarters. They could be a treasure trove of information about the others who weren't as lucky as Caroline."

Lori agreed and started trying to figure out how they would be able to transport these important documents without a box or anything else to put them in.

~ * ~

Doctor Kirsten Jamison studied the information about cryogenics she found on her computer. While she'd been in college, she studied the ancient practice. She'd doubted it was anything more than an urban myth. Now after what Nick and Lori had discovered in the ruins of one of the buildings in what was once Los Angeles, they had debunked the urban myth theory.

Confident she could successfully reverse the process, she prepared to go out to the location where Nick and Lori made the discovery. Her hands shook as she packed her bags with the equipment her research told her would be necessary to reverse the effects of the cryogenics chamber.

Even though she'd never put much stock in the stories about cryogenics, she did recall the stories her grandmother often told her about her great-grandfather's sister, Caroline Lewis. According to what her grandmother told her, Caroline had been distraught over the loss of her husband who had been in China at the outbreak of the 2020 pandemic and died before he could return to the States. At the time she thought she had nothing to live for and went to the cryogenics facility. After her disappearance, the natural disasters began and Kirsten's great-grandfather took his family to the Midwest when the evacuation order had been issued. No one knew what happened to Great Aunt Caroline Lewis. Had she gone through with her plans to be frozen alive or had she lost her life during the disasters? It was one of those family legends that would forever be a mystery.

Outside of her office, her hovercraft pilot waited for her. She knew he wasn't thrilled about flying through the ruins of what was once Los Angeles, but they'd all signed on for this assignment. There were dangers, even mutant animals that roamed the streets of the long-forgotten city, but those were things that archaeologists had been dealing with for years all over the globe. In the past it had been curses on mu-mmies as well as snakes with the venomous bites. These new perils were just as real, forcing everyone who traveled to the area to be well-armed against whatever they might encounter.

"Are you sure you want to go into the inner city, Doctor?"

"That's where Nick and Lori have made the find. I can't very well examine the artifacts if I don't go there myself."

"I understand. I have my laser pistol as well as my rifle loaded, in case we should need to use them. I just hope Nick and Lori are all right. Even though they're armed, they could be in danger."

"From what Nick told me, what they found is in the basement of the ruins of a building. I doubt any animals would be going down a flight of stairs. There certainly isn't any food for them down there. I've heard most of them have retreated to the forests and the mountains."

Her pilot, Alex, nodded his agreement and they took off for the fifteen-minute flight to the area where they knew they would find Nick and Lori.

As they made their way through the now ruined streets of what was once a great city, Kirsten remembered the old pictures she'd found in her grandmother's attic when they cleaned out the house. Some of them were dated during the twentieth century, long before the pandemic or the natural disasters changed life as everyone knew it. The one picture that always drew her back to the old albums was of her great-grandfather, Jonathan Evers, and his sister, the mysterious Caroline Lewis. In the picture was Caroline's husband, Adam, along with great-grandmother Trudy Evers. They stood in front of a large home with well-groomed lawn as well as beds of colorful flowers. The date on the back of the picture was April 2016.

They must have thought they were living in paradise. What a difference those pictures are from the devastation we see now.

The hovercraft landed and parked next to the craft Kirsten knew Nick and Lori took out earlier in the day. The information she received from Nick told her that from here on she would have to go on foot, as there was so much debris there was nowhere closer to park their vehicles.

Alex flanked her as they made their way through the deserted streets of what was once the mecca of the entertainment world. As soon as she saw the sign denoting the cryogenics building, she turned to Alex. "This has to be the place."

Together they went into what had once been the lobby, turned on their flashlights, and made their way to the basement storage room.

"Dr. Jamison, it's good to see you," Nick said.

"I had to see what you have. From the condition of most of these bodies, I can see none of them survived. You did say there was one in perfect condition. Where will I find her?"

Lori got up from her seat at the desk where several three-ring binders were spread out. "She's over here," she said. "We do have a name for her. It's Caroline Lewis. I have all of her information in this binder. They certainly did keep good records on all of the people they put into a state of suspended animation."

"C-Caroline Lewis? Are you sure?"

"Positive. I have all the information on her right here and her name along with the date she was put in the tube is on the front of it. Does it mean something to you?"

"That's the name of my great aunt, the sister of my great-grandfather. I thought the stories about her visiting the cryogenics facility were just that; stories. She disappeared and no one seemed to know whatever happened to her."

Kirsten stepped around Nick and Lori to stare into the face of the woman whose picture had haunted her ever since she found it. Although she appeared older and thinner than the picture, this was definitely her great aunt. She took a deep breath, before she started the procedure she'd researched earlier. If her research was right, Caroline Lewis would slowly awaken, be disoriented, and regain full use of her body within a couple of hours. Of course, they didn't have the luxury of waiting for a couple of hours. Once she was awake, they would have to transport her back to headquarters, where she could be examined under better conditions than the remains of a crumbling building.

"Alex, I want you to help Nick take these binders out to his hovercraft. Lori, you'll have to stay here and help me."

Nick and Alex nodded and started taking armloads of binders back up to where the hovercrafts were parked.

"Did you check to see if there were any other survivors?" Kirsten asked.

"I don't know how it happened, but this was the only chamber that wasn't disturbed. If this is your great aunt, how do you think she'll adjust to waking up fifty years later than she thought she would?"

"Time will tell, but that's something we don't have now. I can reverse the process but it's hard telling if she will wake up immediately. We have to get her back to headquarters as soon as we can. There we have the medical facility to take care of her that we don't have here."

From the notes Lori found in another of the binders, Kirsten started the process to awaken Caroline. There were some tense minutes waiting for the chamber to open. She certainly didn't know what she expected to find. Would the body turn black once the liquid nitrogen was released as had the other bodies, or would the controls take over and prevent something like that from happening. When the proper procedures were put in place, everything should go according to the plans of the original people who ran this facility in 2020.

She listened as the seal released and slowly the lifegiving oxygen reached the lungs of its lone occupant. Kirsten watched as Caroline's chest rose and fell with the breathing she hadn't done in over one hundred years.

Knowing complete awareness would not return for some time, Kirsten waited for Nick and Alex to return. Between the two of them they would have to carry the semi-conscious woman back to where their hovercrafts were parked.

"We put the binders in Nick's craft," Alex said. "Do you want us to make another trip with the rest of them?"

"Lori and I can get them. You need to take Caroline and put her in our hovercraft. We need to get her back to the lab so she can have access to the hospital facilities."

Kirsten watched as Alex and Nick lifted the bed on which Caroline and been lying inside the chamber and used it like a stretcher to transport her out to the hovercraft. Once they were on their way up the stairs, she and Lori picked up the remaining binders and carried them out of the basement. Luckily, they were able to illuminate the darkness with the headlamps on their hardhats while they attached their flashlights to their belts, freeing up their hands.

"That's the last of them, at least from the first drawer. I didn't get into the lower ones."

"I have a feeling there will be other archaeologists coming back here several times in the future, Lori. We can retrieve the rest of the files later or even send out another team to bring them back to headquarters. For now, I'm anxious to get Aunt Caroline back where she can be made comfortable."

Other Books by the Author
at
Rogue Phoenix Press

The Return of the Ancients
The Aliens Book One

Nina is devastated when she realizes she must leave Plantas along with the man who is to become her mate, Ragnar, and her best friend, Tarena. When Nina arrives on Earth in Peru at the Nazca plains, she is greeted by a young archaeology student, Rand Jacobson. Even though she is attracted to Rand, she is still grieving the loss of Ragnar.

Ragnar is surprised when, after being greeted as a god on the planet Seros, the military opens fire on his family. After being taken prisoner, he is treated like a lab rat until a scientist, Geni, comes to his rescue. At her estate, he learns the physicians who work with her have saved the lives of his family and friends.

My Uncle the King
The Aliens Book Two

When three contingencies took off from their dying planet, Plantas, only two arrived at their destination unharmed. When the lost contingency is hit with a meteor storm, only one ship survives and makes it to their destination of Nalo. Over the generations, the descendants of the original refugees become the ruling class of their adopted planet. Even the rebel group, the Pure Of Nalo, are unable to unseat the monarchy. When relations with Earth are established, it is Prince Nicos who leaves Nalo to find love on an alien planet and bring back new ideas as well as his Earthly family to save the throne and the people of Nalo.

You Again

While attending college at the University of Wisconsin in the 1960s, Carole Martinson fell in love and eloped with Phillip Vanderlin. When his parents realized she was a farmer's daughter and below them socially, they insisted they divorce.

Fast forward to 2019 and Carole is invited to a wedding cruise financed by her granddaughter's fiancé's grandfather. With no knowledge about the groom's family, Carole flies to Florida for the cruise she and her second husband never got to take. Upon her arrival, she immediately recognizes Phillip.

Phillip never forgot his first love. He is thrilled when he realizes the grandmother is the girl he was forced to leave behind so many years ago.

www.ingramcontent.com/pod-product-compliance
Lightning Source LLC
Chambersburg PA
CBHW060045150626
46556CB00018BA/2702